PROLOGUE

'They called me a murderess,' said the girl's ghostly voice. 'Then they killed me, because I knew too much. Now you must prove my innocence – or you too will die, just as I did!'

Cassie awoke choking, with the feel of thin ghostly fingers clamped round her throat . . .

She sat up with a strangled cry of alarm, waving her arms wildly. The fingers disappeared, but she could still sense an angry presence somewhere in the room.

Just for a moment she saw a thin pale figure standing by the window. Then it faded away . . .

3

CHAPTER ONE

HAUNTED

It was a sunny summer morning, I was strolling along a Cornish cliff-top path with Cassie, and everything was right with the world. And if that sounds too good to be true – it is!

I should have known it couldn't last. There was trouble, big trouble, on the way.

I'm Ben Harker and Cassie is Cassandra Sinclair. We both go to St John's Academy, a school for the children of the disgustingly rich in the City of London.

Cassie qualifies because of her mother, a high-powered corporation lawyer. My entry ticket is my dad, a self-made tycoon who built an East End fruit stall into a chain of companies.

4

Cassie and I met not long ago when she came to St John's and we hit it off straight away. We had a lot in common, both only children in single-parent families. Mum cleared off when I was still a baby and I live with Dad in a block of luxury flats not far from school. Cassie lives with her mother in the same block of flats. Her parents are still married but live separate lives.

We were a long way from the City of London right now. Cassie's mother had taken a big old house in Cornwall for the summer at a place called Doombar Bay. I'd been invited to stay for a few weeks. Cassie and her mother had holidayed in the area before. Despite its sinister name, Doombar Bay is an exceptionally beautiful spot. The small sandy bay, surrounded by towering cliffs, makes a great family beach.

The house we were staying in, called, naturally enough, Doombar House, stood alone on the cliffs that overlook the bay. It was a massive old-fashioned place, shabby but comfortable, with lots more rooms than the three of us needed. I wondered why Cassie's mother had chosen it, but it seemed rude to ask.

We'd spent the last couple of days on the beach at Doombar Bay. Today, just for a change, we'd turned right instead of left coming out of the house. We were having an after-breakfast stroll along the cliff-top path that led to the nearest town, Polzod. To our right were heather-covered fields, to our left a sheer drop. Far below, waves crashed against jagged rocks, sending clouds of foaming spray high into the air.

I glanced at Cassie, who was staring out to sea. As always, she looked terrific. Long blonde hair, a high forehead, huge green eyes . . . Thin, you might even say skinny, but graceful with it. She looked like a model – even in old khaki shorts and a faded T-shirt!

So, everything was cool – except that Cassie was in a weird mood. She'd been worried and upset all through breakfast, and she was the same now.

Cassie has a trick of knowing what I'm thinking. Suddenly she stopped and looked up at me.

'Ben . . .'

'What?'

For a moment Cassie didn't reply.

'Come on, out with it,' I said. 'Something's been bugging you all morning.'

'Our holiday house is haunted.'

'What makes you think so?'

'I saw a ghost last night.'

'You would!' I said. I saw an unhappy look flash across her face and added a quick, 'Sorry!'

The thing is, there's more to Cassie than just good looks. She has the gift – or as Cassie herself thinks of it, the curse – of second sight. She gets flashes of the future, often warnings of disaster. She can read people, tell if they're genuine or working some kind of con. She sees and feels things the rest of us miss.

Like I said, she feels it's more of a curse than a blessing. Sometimes she sees more than she wants to – like a ghost!

'Sorry,' I said again. 'You know what I mean. What happened exactly?'

'I woke up with somebody strangling me,' said Cassie. 'And I heard a voice, a girl's voice. She said something about being called a murderess – and being killed herself, because she knew too much. She said I had to prove her innocence, or I'd die too.'

'Nasty,' I said. 'What happened next?'

'I sat up in bed and gave a sort of strangled squawk and the fingers faded away.'

'Did you see anything?'

'Yes, I did,' said Cassie seriously. 'Just for a moment there was a shape standing by the window. A girl in some kind of white gown. Then it disappeared.'

I put an arm round her shoulders and gave her a hug. 'No wonder you looked a bit upset over breakfast!'

Cassie nodded. 'And I'll tell you something else – I'm not looking forward to bedtime either.'

'We could swap rooms,' I suggested.

'I doubt if it would help. Ghosts can walk through walls!'

'I could spend the night with you in your room – in an armchair, or on the floor.'

Cassie grinned. 'I doubt if Mum would care for that.'

She was right. Cassie's mother was a thoroughly modern Ms most of the time, but about some things she was *very* old-fashioned.

'We'll both sit up, downstairs.'

'Maybe,' said Cassie. 'Let's see how I feel by tonight.'

'Are you going to tell your mother?'

Cassie shook her head. 'No, she'll only worry. You know how she is about that sort of thing.'

Cassie's mother had a funny attitude to her daughter's gift. She couldn't really handle the problem, so she pretended it didn't exist. She knew and didn't know all at the same time.

We carried on walking.

I walked along without saying anything, thinking over Cassie's story. The trouble with things that go bump in the night, I told myself, was that night always comes. Right now it was a bright sunny morning, to be followed, I hoped, by a nice sunny afternoon.

There was lots of interesting stuff for us to do. But whatever we did, sooner or later it was going to get dark . . .

Cassie would have to face the night in the old, dark house on the cliff-top. A house haunted by a ghost that was threatening to kill her . . .

I turned to look at Cassie to see how she was doing and discovered she wasn't there. She'd branched off from the path and was headed for a V-shaped cleft in the cliff-top. She was running towards the cliff-edge . . .

'Cassie, come back!' I yelled.

She ignored me.

I started sprinting towards her, and reached her just as she got to the edge of the cliff. I grabbed the back of her T-shirt and tried to pull her back. I stopped her moving forwards, but I couldn't move her away – and she was still dangerously close to the crumbling cliff-edge. I flung my arms round her waist, and heaved. It was like trying to move an iron post.

Over her shoulder I could see the waves smashing on the jagged rocks that filled the base of the cleft.

I yelled into Cassie's ear. 'Cassie, pack it up, come back. You'll get us both killed!'

Cassie's voice was cold and strange. 'I have to go to her. She's calling me. Can't you see her?'

I stared into the clouds of spray, and just for a moment I thought I saw a shape . . .

Whatever it was, I wanted nothing to do with it. With one last desperate effort, I tightened my grip on Cassie's waist and threw myself violently backwards, carrying Cassie with me. We both rolled over on to the springy turf. I ended up on top of her, and grabbed her shoulders, pinning her down before she could start her lemming act again.

'Cassie, what's going on? Are you all right?'

She stared fixedly at me for a moment, and I even thought about slapping her. Then her face cleared and she was more or less herself again.

'It's all right, Ben,' she said shakily. 'I'm OK now.'

She didn't look OK to me. She was trembling and gasping, her face was chalk-white, and her eyes were wide with fear.

I got up and helped her to her feet, taking care to keep between her and the cliff-edge.

'You two want to be careful, larking about like that,' said a disapproving voice behind us.

We turned and saw a man standing on the path. He wore baggy khaki shorts and a faded striped T-shirt. His hair was white and his bald forehead was tanned a deep brown. He had bright blue eyes and a weathered, wrinkled face. A stubby black pipe jutted from his mouth, and an ancient Labrador on a lead lay at his feet, panting from the heat.

'Sorry,' I said. 'My friend got too close to the edge and I got worried. I was just pulling her away.'

He puffed on his pipe. 'Most dangerous place on the cliffs, that is.' There was a soft local burr in his voice.

He pointed reprovingly to a faded noticeboard near by.

It read: *Doombar Point. Unstable Area. Keep Away From Cliff-Edge.*

'Proper name's Doombar Point, but they call it Maiden's Leap.'

'Why? *Why do they call it that?*' asked Cassie urgently. She still looked pretty shaken, but she was fighting to get a grip on herself.

'Some poor maid killed herself there,' said the man with gruesome relish. 'Threw herself over the edge. Waves picked her up and smashed her down on the rocks, time and again. They say there wasn't much left of her.' He gave us a stern look. 'Anybody goes over the cliff just there is as good as dead.'

Cassie shivered. 'When did all this happen?' she asked.

'Years ago; I were just a lad.'

Cassie made a big effort and gave him her most charming smile.

'It's a fascinating story. I don't mean to be rude, but – how old are you?'

If anything the old boy seemed flattered by her question.

'I'm sixty-five this year, my lovely,' he said proudly. 'Just started collecting me old age pension – what there is of it!'

'And how old were you when all this happened – when you were a lad?'

He thought for a moment, puffing his pipe.

'That's hard to say. It was a terrible long time ago.'

Cassie gave him another smile. 'Please try!'

He thought it over a bit more and said, 'It was the year I left school to work with Dad on the lobster pots. I'd be about fifteen . . .' He sighed, looking into the distant past. 'Well, I'd best be on my way.' He looked down at the old Labrador. 'Come on, boy.'

The old dog staggered to its feet.

'Goodbye,' I said. 'Thanks for warning us about Maiden's Leap.'

He nodded, and he and his dog went on their way.

I turned to Cassie. 'It looks like we've found your ghost!'

'I know,' said Cassie. She looked back towards Maiden's Leap and shivered.

'Look, what happened just now?' I asked. 'You seemed to be in some kind of trance.'

'I suppose I was,' said Cassie. 'All I know is, I suddenly felt something *pulling* me. When I got to the cliff-edge I *saw* her, there in the clouds of spray. She was calling me, telling me to join her . . .'

I nodded. 'She must have been the maiden who took the leap.'

'What about the part about her committing suicide?' said Cassie. 'My ghost said she was killed, murdered.'

'Killed because she knew too much,' I reminded her. 'Maybe she didn't commit suicide after all. Maybe she knew the real murderer and he put her out of the way.'

Cassie frowned. 'Murdered her and then faked a suicide? Could he have got away with it?'

I nodded. 'Wouldn't be too hard. Knock her out, shove her over the cliff . . .'

Cassie shuddered. After a moment she said, 'It was all so long ago. How can we find out what really happened after all this time?'

'There are ways,' I said.

'Such as?'

'The ancient mariner says he's sixty-five.'

'So?'

'Well, the murder happened when he was fifteen.'

Even I could manage that much mental arithmetic. 'So that's –'

'Fifty years ago,' said Cassie.

'Right! So the murder, if there was one, happened in . . .'

'1951,' said Cassie. 'And it was actually two murders, remember. She said she was accused of being a murderess – so somebody, somebody else, must have been murdered first. And if her suicide was really a murder as well . . .'

'Two murders, then,' I said. 'One disguised as a suicide. There can't have been that many gruesome murder-suicides in this part of Cornwall in 1951. There's bound to be a record somewhere.' I looked at my watch. 'Want to head back for lunch?'

Cassie shook her head. 'I've gone off Doombar House. Let's walk on into Polzod and get something there.'

I looked at her in horror. 'Walk to Polzod? It's miles away!'

'Only about three. Do you good.'

'Your mother's expecting us back for lunch.'

'I'll give Mum a ring.' Cassie tapped the tiny mobile phone in the pocket of her shorts. Her mother always insisted on her carrying one. 'She won't mind, she'll probably be working anyway.'

Cassie's mother didn't really understand the idea of holidays. She'd been busy on her laptop ever since we'd arrived. Cassie had an idea she was working on some local property deal.

She phoned her mother then and there. Mrs Sinclair was quite happy about our staying out for lunch. Probably glad to be rid of us.

'She'd like us to be back fairly early though,' said Cassie when she'd finished her call. 'Apparently the local squire has invited us for drinks.'

I groaned. 'Me as well?'

'Of course. Mum will have told him you're our guest; it would be rude to leave you behind. Besides, you don't want to spend the evening alone with the ghost, do you?'

Maybe she had a point.

We walked on towards the little town, but there was an unseen shadow over the sunny day. Sooner or later we'd have to go back to the old dark house on the cliffs, and face whatever was waiting for us in the night.

SEARCH FOR THE PAST

After far too long a walk – for me, anyway – we rounded the curve of the headland. We found ourselves looking down on Polzod Bay, with the little town of Polzod huddled behind it. The bay itself curves round in a huge crescent, floored with a flat downward-sloping beach. Long straight waves crash in from the sea, which makes the place ideal for surfing – and surfing is what Polzod is all about.

The bay below was full of happy surfers, paddling their little boards out to sea and riding the waves back to the beach. I couldn't see the point myself, but there was no doubt that surfing was terrifically popular. The shops that lined the bay sold, or hired, wetsuits, surfboards of every shape and size and every other kind of surfing gear. Half a dozen beach-side cafés sold hot dogs, hamburgers and fish and chips, to feed the hungry surfers. The smell of hot fat floated up to the cliff-top.

We looked down at the swarming figures on the beach and Cassie said, 'I'd like to try that some time, it looks fun.'

If Cassie's got one fault, it's that she's too keen on healthy exercise. Tennis, badminton, basketball – and long healthy walks.

I'm more the armchair type myself, though I sometimes stagger through the odd scratch soccer game.

I shook my head. 'You're mad!'

'And you're lazy!' said Cassie.

'Dead right,' I said. 'I'm already worn out by all that walking. Let's have a sit-down and a can of Coke.'

There was a combined café and shop close by on the cliff-top. Not much more than a shack, it sold ice-cream, soft drinks, snacks and sweets – and surfboards of course. I bought a couple of cans of Coke and we sat down at one of the rusty iron tables outside.

For a moment we drank our Cokes in silence. Then Cassie said, 'So, what are we going to do about my ghost?'

I yawned and stretched. 'We could try exorcising it – bell, book and candle and all that. Maybe we can find a nice helpful vicar. Or we could just catch the next train back to London.'

'And leave Mum here alone?'

'She wouldn't see it – she doesn't believe in such things. Besides, no ghost would haunt her – it wouldn't dare!'

'No,' said Cassie determinedly. 'I don't want to run away. I want to help her.'

I stared at her in amazement. 'Help the ghost? Help an evil spirit that threatened to kill you?'

'I don't believe she's evil, not really.'

'Even though she tried to throttle you?'

'She didn't *feel* evil,' said Cassie obstinately. 'Just desperate – and tormented. After all, if your theory's right, she had a rotten deal. Accused of a murder she didn't commit, then murdered herself. We've got to help her, Ben.'

She gave me an appealing look with those big green eyes. I couldn't resist that look and she knew it.

'All right,' I said. 'What do you want to do?'

'Find out more about the crime – crimes.' She looked hopefully at me. 'You said yourself there'd be some kind of record.'

'I could try the Internet,' I said. 'Or somebody

might have recorded it in one of those true crime books. People love a nice gruesome murder.' A sudden thought struck me. 'Hang on . . .'

'What?'

'It must have been in all the papers. Well, it would be, wouldn't it? Must have been a big sensation locally, especially back in the Fifties. Newspaper files, that's what we need.'

'Do they keep them that far back?'

'They might. We'll try the newspaper offices in town. Come on!'

Swigging the last of my Coke, I jumped to my feet.

We walked down the steep lane that led to the sea front, and followed the broad road that curved around the bay. The beach was filled with hairy-chested, golden-tanned surfers, taking a break before plunging back into the waves. They all seemed to be seven feet tall and bulging with muscles.

We went into a newsagent and checked out the local papers. There were only two, a modern-looking tabloid called the *Polzod Pioneer*, and a more old-fashioned-looking publication, the *Polzod Bugle*. The *Bugle*'s masthead bore the words *Founded 1910*.

'This is the one for us,' I said. We bought a copy and I asked the man in the shop where its offices were. He directed me to a street in the old town, which lay behind the beach.

The offices of the *Polzod Bugle* were behind an old-fashioned shop-front, the kind that has a curved bottle-glass window. Inside was a cramped reception area with a high wooden counter. Behind the counter sat a pretty blonde-haired girl reading a magazine. Except for the computer on her desk, it looked as if nothing much had changed since 1910.

It seemed to be a quiet news day on the *Polzod Bugle*.

The girl looked up as we came in, as if pleased to have some visitors to break the monotony.

'Can I help you?' Her voice had the soft Cornish burr. 'Want to put an ad in the classifieds, do you? Rates are . . .' She began to rattle off a list of prices, but I interrupted her.

'No, it's not that. We're doing a project on local history and we wondered if we could have a quick look at your back-files.'

She thought for a moment. 'Don't see why not. Nothing much going on today.' She grinned. 'Nothing much going on any day, to be honest.' She swung her chair round to face the computer. 'We put them all on computer a while back. I'll see if I can just punch them up for you.'

Her red-nailed fingers flashed over the keyboard, and after a moment she swung the computer round so we could see the screen. It was filled with the miniaturised front page of an old-fashioned newspaper.

'There you are,' she said proudly. 'Right back to 1910!'

'Could you possibly look up 1951 for us?' asked Cassie.

Fingers rattled over the keyboard, for longer this time, then the girl looked up in surprise. 'There's nothing between 1950 and 1952. You've asked for the one year we haven't got!'

'How can that have happened?' I asked.

She shrugged. 'Search me! Maybe someone erased it accidentally. See, the files used to be kept in great big leather-bound books, down in the basement. Piles of them there were, going back to 1910. You can imagine how much space that took up! They wanted the basement for storage so they put all the files on the computer.'

'What happened to all the leather-bound books?' I asked.

'I think they gave them to the library, over in George Street.'

'Right, we'll try –'

A door behind the counter opened, and a sharp-faced, fussy-looking man in a shabby suit appeared. He looked at the computer screen in outrage.

'What's going on here, Miss Pollard?' he snapped.

'These young people asked to see our back-files, Mr Trefusis, and I didn't see any harm. Funnily enough they wanted to see the 1951 file, but that one seems to be missing.'

He leaned forward and stabbed at the keyboard and the screen went blank.

'The proprietor has ordered that all newspaper files are strictly confidential. I'll speak to you later.'

The girl flounced away, and Mr Trefusis turned to us. 'As for you two, you should know better than to make unauthorised enquiries. These things must be done through the proper channels. I must ask for your names and addresses.'

'Why?' I asked. 'We asked your paper for help, but you've screwed up your own files and can't give it. That ends it.'

I don't think he was used to being talked to like that. He went an alarming shade of purple and shouted, 'I will not tolerate insolence! I insist on knowing who you are and why –'

I felt Cassie tugging at my sleeve.

'Insist all you like,' I said. 'Good morning.'

We went out of the office.

I looked back as we went into the street and saw him glaring furiously after us. He snatched up a phone.

'Why didn't you want to give him our names?' asked Cassie as we walked towards George Street.

I shrugged. 'Didn't seem any point. Besides, I didn't like his manner.'

'You were quite right,' said Cassie. 'I could feel something evil about him. Something sly and treacherous.'

I told you she could read people.

We headed for the library.

It was a big place for such a little town, an imposing Roman-style building with pillars beside the door and a flight of steps. Inside was a marble-floored foyer with doors leading off. Over one of them in faded gold lettering were the words REFERENCE LIBRARY.

We went inside and found ourselves in a long, gloomy room filled with rows of highly-polished mahogany tables and chairs, each with its own reading lamp.

There was a mahogany counter to the left of the door. Behind it, a little old lady with gold-rimmed granny-glasses and her white hair in a bun sat dozing on a stool. Apart from her the place was completely deserted.

I guess surfers don't do much research.

I coughed discreetly and the old lady came to life.

'Good morning,' she said sweetly. 'Can I help you?'

I showed her my copy of the *Polzod Bugle*. 'We'd like to look at the back-files of this paper, if that's possible.'

'Oh yes,' she said proudly. 'We have them all here, right back to the very first issue, January 1910! There they are, up there.' She pointed to a shelf of enormous leather-bound volumes high up at the back of her counter. Each one had a year stamped in gold lettering on the spine. 'Which year are you interested in?'

'1951, please,' I said.

Just for a moment the old lady seemed to freeze. Then she climbed on to a set of library steps and peered along the row. '1949, 1950, 1952 – oh dear! 1951 seems to be missing. It must be out on loan.' She came down the ladder. 'We do lend them out occasionally, local historians, people like that. I'll just check for you.'

She reached under the counter and fished out a dusty ledger.

'Ah yes, here we are. 1951 is out on loan to a local historian. Would any other year be of use to you?'

'I'm afraid not,' said Cassie.

'Indeed? And just why are you so interested in that particular year?'

She still spoke in that sweet-little-old-lady voice,

but there was a keen edge of curiosity beneath it.

I produced the usual story. 'We're doing a special project for our school magazine,' I said vaguely. 'Do you think your historian would let us take a quick look at the 1951 files? We wouldn't need them for very long.'

Cassie picked up her cue. 'Is he local? We could go and see him.'

'I don't think he would care for that,' said the old lady firmly. 'He's very much of a recluse.' She frowned at the ledger. 'However, he has had the files for some time. I'll telephone him and ask if he still needs them. If he's finished with them I'm sure he'll return them. Are you staying here long?'

'A couple of weeks,' I said.

'Give me your names, phone numbers and addresses and I'll let you know what he says.'

Before I could reply, Cassie said quickly, 'No, please don't bother. We often come into Polzod. We'll call in a day or so and you can tell us if there's any news.'

She grabbed my arm and started dragging me out of the reading-room. I turned to say goodbye to the old lady and found that she was on the telephone, a sharp, concentrated expression on her face. Suddenly she didn't look so sweet any more. We crossed the echoing foyer and went down the library steps.

'She was lying,' said Cassie when we were back in

the street. 'The whole thing was a performance.'

First the man in the newspaper office and now the old lady. Cassie's psychic powers were working full blast.

'She knew the 1951 file wasn't there all along,' Cassie went on. 'She just wanted to find out who we were.'

'Why?'

'Because she's interested in anyone who wants to know what happened here in 1951.'

'Maybe she's the murderer,' I said mockingly.

'Maybe she is,' said Cassie. 'Who knows what she was like fifty years ago! Or maybe she knows who the murderer is.'

I stared at her. 'Are you serious?'

'I told you, there's something sinister about her – I could feel it. She's not nearly as sweet and innocent as she looks!'

'Oh sure! She probably had a machine-gun under her counter, and poisoned spikes in her boots.'

'Someone's been seeing too many James Bond films,' said Cassie. 'Come on, let's find some lunch.'

'All right. But can we find somewhere quiet, away from the beach? All those hairy great beach-boys ruin my appetite.'

Cassie grinned. 'You're jealous! Just because you haven't got a hairy chest and a gold medallion . . . You should take up body-building.'

'And end up looking like a condom full of walnuts?'

Cassie looked shocked. 'What?'

I grinned at her. 'Just quoting. It's what some film critic called Arnie Schwarzenegger – or was it Sylvester Stallone?'

As we wandered through the narrow streets of the old town, quieter and more pleasant than the noisy beach, I couldn't help wondering about the old lady.

Even though I'd made a joke of it, I was sure that Cassie was right. Her special 'feelings' about people were always spot on. Besides, I'd picked up on something odd about the old lady's manner myself towards the end. And the man in the newspaper office had lost it for no good reason. But where did they fit into a mystery that involved two fifty-year-old murders and a vengeful ghost?

I saw a nice-looking little pub at the end of a cobbled alley and pointed it out to Cassie. It had wooden tables and benches outside, and flowering plants in big wooden tubs beside the door.

'How about that place?'

'Will they serve us?'

'Sure – as long as we don't order two large whiskies!'

We walked up to the pub and Cassie sat at one of the tables.

27

'Ham sandwiches, or cheese?' I asked.

'Both,' said Cassie. 'I'm starving!'

For such a skinny girl she's got a very healthy appetite.

I went inside the pub, blinking in its cool shadows after the sunshine outside. An enormous man, barrel chest straining against a striped T-shirt, stood on the other side of the bar. A handful of drinkers, mostly elderly, sat sipping their pints of ale at a scattering of little tables.

I bought two Cokes, and ordered two plates of sandwiches, one ham and one cheese. I carried the Cokes outside. We sat drinking and chatting, and after a while the big landlord brought the sandwiches.

We polished off both plates in no time, and I went into the pub to get two more Cokes.

As I came out again, I saw three youngish men walking down the alley. They came right up to the pub and stood in a semi-circle surrounding Cassie.

I put the Cokes down on a table and studied them carefully.

They looked like trouble. Bad trouble.

All three wore dirty jeans and scruffy T-shirts and all three had a distinctly thuggish air. The one in the middle, who seemed to be the leader, was big and brawny with long greasy black hair, an unsuccessful moustache and a stubbly chin. The one on his left was tall and skinny with a shaven head. The one to his right was smaller, mean and ratty-looking, with a bristly crew-cut.

I walked over beside Cassie and looked down at her. 'Friends of yours?' I said.

I made a big effort to keep my voice as calm as possible.

Cassie was obviously doing the same thing. 'Never saw them before. They turned up at the end of the alley, just after you went inside.'

I looked at the ugly trio, wondering what they were after. Had they simply seen Cassie sitting alone outside the pub and decided to hassle her for the fun of it? Or was something more sinister going on?

The big yob in the middle didn't like the way we were ignoring them. Suddenly he jabbed me hard in the chest with a grimy finger. It hurt.

'We got a message for you, sonny – for the both of you.'

I drew a deep breath, struggling to keep calm. I thought about yelling to the landlord for help, but I didn't want to risk making things worse. I was hoping they'd just been sent to threaten us. As far as I was concerned they could threaten all they liked. 'Words can't hurt me,' as the saying goes. I was just keen to stop things getting to the sticks and stones and breaking bones stage.

It wasn't that I was scared – more like terrified, actually – it was a simple question of being practical. There were three of them and one of me. I know a bit of basic judo, enough to save my skin in a playground fight. But I wasn't kidding myself. It's only in Jackie Chan movies that someone takes on three opponents and wins. This was real life.

'All right,' I said, trying to keep the quiver out of my voice. 'Go ahead.'

The thug seemed confused. 'You what?'

'You said you had a message for us. Let's hear it.'

'Yeah, right.' He frowned, struggling to remember what he'd clearly been told to say. He twisted his ugly face in a ferocious scowl. 'Stop raking up old dirt, interfering in stuff that's none of your business. There's people round here who don't like it, and they can turn very nasty. This is a warning, see, and it's the only one you get! Understood? Or do you want it the hard way?'

He grabbed the front of my shirt and drew back a massive fist . . .

CHAPTER THREE

PUNCH-UP

With another mighty effort, I managed to keep my voice low and calm.

'No, I don't want it the hard way. And yes, I do understand. We won't ask any more questions and we'll leave right away.'

The thug seemed disappointed. 'You sure?' He gave me a shake that rattled my teeth.

'Quite sure, thank you.'

He sneered contemptuously and released his grip, turning away.

Just for a moment I thought we'd got away with it.

Then Cassie bounded to her feet and yelled, 'Leave him alone, you big ape!'

The thug swung round on her. 'You're a lively little piece, ain't you?' he said, almost admiringly. 'Don't worry, we won't hurt your boyfriend. How about a goodbye kiss, just to show there's no hard feelings?'

He reached out and stroked her face.

Cassie slapped his hand aside with her left hand, drew back her right arm and hit him very hard on the end of the nose with a small bony fist. She's a lot stronger than she looks. Must be all that basketball and tennis.

The big thug must have had an extra-sensitive nose. A fountain of blood gushed out, soaking the front of his grimy white T-shirt. He staggered back, stunned, staring in disbelief at his bloody shirt. He touched his nose tenderly, smearing more blood over his face.

'Bitch!' he yelled and made for Cassie.

Quickly I moved between them. If I could throw him while he was still distracted by the nosebleed . . .

A voice shouted, 'Oy!'

The big landlord came out of the pub and everybody froze. He looked at the blood-soaked thug and his two mates.

'What's going on?'

'No idea,' I said. 'These three turned up and that one started hassling my friend.'

'So you hit him?' said the landlord approvingly.

'No, she did!'

I grinned at Cassie, who was standing there wide-eyed, as if astonished at what she'd done. I put an arm round her shoulders.

Then the number two thug, the tall skinhead, decided to join in.

'I wouldn't interfere if I was you, mate. Something might happen to that nice little pub of yours.'

Casually, the landlord clipped his ear. The skinhead staggered three paces sideways, and then crashed over one of the heavy wooden tables, collapsing on the other side.

He scrambled to his feet, his face ugly.

The big thug wiped the blood from his face and seemed about to charge.

I'd leave him to the landlord I decided, and do my best to tackle the skinhead. The odds were improving but things still looked tricky. I glanced at the ratty-looking one, who was already edging towards the alley, and decided he could be ignored.

Suddenly two men strolled down the alley. They were obviously the landlord's sons. They looked exactly like him – only bigger.

'Everything all right, Dad?' said one of them.

'Yeah, just a bit of a dust-up with the local riff-raff.'

The ratty thug had already vanished, and the land-lord turned to the two others.

'I recognise you lot. You're with that gang of yobs who hang about down the arcade. You're barred; if I see you again, you're for it. Now, 'oppit!'

They hopped it, the thin one limping from his fall, the big one dabbing at his bloody face.

The landlord turned to us. 'You two all right?'

'Just about,' I said. 'Look, do you think you could call us a taxi? I don't fancy running into those three again – and they may have friends.'

The landlord dropped a ham-like hand on my shoulder. 'Don't you worry, young fella,' he said. 'If there's any trouble, little missy here will look after you . . .'

We sat in the back of the ancient taxi, jolting back towards Doombar House. For a while neither of us said anything; we were both pretty shaken. I was just glad we'd escaped in one piece.

Cassie squeezed my arm. 'You were wonderful, Ben. So calm.'

'Only on the outside. I was just trying to stop it turning into a fight we couldn't win.'

'And I ruined it all!'

'It's all this feminism,' I said gloomily. 'Don't you

know the heroine's just supposed to scream and get rescued by the hero? These days the hero stands there and does nothing while the heroine beats up the villains.'

'I'm sorry, Ben.'

'Never mind. Luckily the landlord arrived in time.'

'It was all so weird,' said Cassie. 'I mean, who sent them?'

I nodded towards the taxi-driver and shook my head warningly. We finished the journey in silence. I asked the driver to drop us at the end of the lane and paid him off. We watched him drive away.

Cassie shook her head. 'This is getting more like a Bond film all the time!'

'No point in taking chances,' I said. 'It's a small town, and you never know who's talking to who.'

She nodded. 'So who do you think sent those yobs after us?'

'That bloke Trefusis at the newspaper, probably. Either him or the old lady in the library. Who else knew we were interested in what happened round here back in 1951?'

'Right,' said Cassie. 'We only decided to try and find out ourselves this morning.'

'They both got on the telephone as soon as we started to leave,' I said. 'They must have called someone, told them what had happened, given them

35

our description. That someone sent those three out to look for us.'

'Bit of a long shot, surely?'

'Not really. Like I said, it's not that big a town. And for all we know they might have had several teams out looking.'

'I think you're right,' said Cassie thoughtfully. 'Just after you went inside the pub, those three turned up at the end of the alley and stood staring at me for a few minutes. I thought it was just because I was a girl and on my own. Then they started to move on. When you came out of the pub they changed their minds and came after us.'

'They were looking for a couple, working from a description someone had given them. The question is, who's the someone?'

'Somebody powerful,' said Cassie. 'Rich and powerful probably, the two go together.'

'A master-criminal? The Godfather of Polzod?'

'I don't think so,' said Cassie. 'Not necessarily.'

'Why not? Anyone who can whistle up a gang of thugs at a moment's notice . . .'

'Maybe our somebody knew another somebody,' said Cassie. 'Passed the order down the line.'

'What makes you so sure it's not a crook we're after?'

'It's hard to explain . . . Look, we're enquiring into an old scandal, right? And the minute we start, *before* we start, someone's desperate to scare us off.'

'So?'

'A real crook wouldn't *care* about old scandals. I think we're after someone respectable, outwardly at least. Someone who can't afford a scandal.'

'Aha!' I said. 'A picture is emerging! All we have to do now is check up on all the local bigwigs.'

'We can start tonight,' said Cassie. 'We're having drinks with the Squire, remember?'

Cassie's mother was waiting for us when we got back to Doombar House. She was wearing what I suppose you'd call a little black dress and some kind of filmy scarf. The sort of outfit that looks so simple you know it must have cost a fortune.

'There you are! You've just got time to bath and change before we leave.'

I opened my mouth to groan, but Cassie gave me a stern look and an elbow-jab in the ribs.

'All right, Mum,' she said. 'But it had better be worth it. Who are we dressing up for?'

'A man called Richard Daumier. He's a very important man round here, lots of business interests. That's why they call him the Squire.'

The name sounded vaguely familiar. Suddenly I realised why. It was on half of the shops and businesses in Polzod. Daumier's Bakers, Daumier's Boatyard, Daumier's Supermarket . . .

Cassie surveyed her mother's outfit. 'He must be important if you've got the Balenciaga out. And the Prada shoes.'

'He is,' said Mrs Sinclair. 'And as a matter of fact . . .' She broke off, looking a little shamefaced.

'Come on, Mum, out with it,' said Cassie. 'I know you didn't come all the way down here just for sun, sea and sandcastles.'

Mrs Sinclair did her best to look dignified. 'As it happens, I'm representing Mr Daumier's interests in an important case. So I'd be grateful if you'd both try to make a good impression!'

'What sort of case?' I asked, just to be polite.

'It's a matter of contesting the provisions of a family trust,' she said vaguely.

'Why does he want to contest it?' asked Cassie.

For a moment her mother didn't reply.

'Come on,' said Cassie. 'What's going on? Something is, I can always tell. You've got your shifty lawyer's look on.'

'All right,' said her mother reluctantly. 'But I must ask you both to keep it confidential.'

'We will,' said Cassie. 'Go on.'

'Mr Daumier owns this house, and much of the cliff-top land around it. The trust was set up back in the Thirties. It forbids him to sell the land, or even to develop it in any way. If we can overturn the trust, all this land will become immensely valuable . . .'

'And this lovely cliff will be lined with bungalows,' said Cassie angrily. 'Mum, how could you!'

'There may be some property development, yes,' said Mrs Sinclair. 'Not bungalows, but good quality residential housing. You know I share your concern for the environment, Cassandra, but . . .'

'But business is business?' said Cassie.

'That's right,' said Mrs Sinclair. 'Business is business.'

The two glared angrily at each other.

'Maybe it's time we went and got changed?' I suggested.

Cassie turned and stalked out of the room.

'Oh dear,' said Mrs Sinclair. 'Do your best to calm her down, will you, Ben? If she starts being difficult tonight . . .'

'I'll try,' I said, and followed Cassie out of the room.

I caught up with her at the bottom of the big old staircase.

'Don't be too hard on your mum, Cassie,' I said as

we climbed it together. 'She's only doing her job.'

'I know,' said Cassie angrily. 'It's just that some-times – well, she just doesn't seem to have a conscience.'

I looked at her in mock-surprise. 'Of course not – she's a lawyer!'

We reached the gloomy landing at the top of the stairs and paused.

'Your mother's afraid you'll tick Daumier off for being a wicked property developer,' I said.

'She needn't worry,' said Cassie. 'I shall be on my best behaviour tonight.'

'Doesn't sound like you,' I said. 'Why?'

'This Daumier might be the man we're after.'

'What makes you say that?'

'He fits the profile, doesn't he? Local bigwig and all that?'

'I suppose so. But there could be dozens of others who fit the profile just as well.'

'Maybe. But since this is the one we're having drinks with, we may as well start with him.' She paused for a moment and then went on, 'And I'll tell you something else, Ben, something we've overlooked. It's so obvious, I don't know why we didn't see it before.'

'What's that?'

'This is where I first saw the ghost, here in this house . . . And aren't ghosts supposed to haunt the scene of the crime – the actual place where they were killed?'

I nodded slowly. 'That's the tradition. Which means . . .'

'Exactly,' said Cassie. 'The murder of the girl, and perhaps the murder she was accused of, probably happened right here in this house – which belongs to Richard Daumier.'

'You saw the ghost at Maiden's Leap as well,' I reminded her.

Cassie thought for a moment. 'Maybe the first murder, the one she was accused of, happened here. Perhaps she was killed at Maiden's Leap and thrown over the edge. Either way, this house was concerned in the murders. There may still be some clues here.'

'Like a signed confession from the real murderer?'

'Who knows? Tomorrow we'll search the place, attics to cellars. We could do it now if it wasn't for this silly drinks party.'

'Which we'll be late for if we don't get a move on,' I said.

We met downstairs half an hour later, all clean and tidy. Mrs Sinclair surveyed us critically. 'I suppose you'll do.'

Cassie was wearing a dark blue dress I'd seen her in before. She looked terrific, and I told her so.

She blushed and looked pleased. 'You look great too, Ben.'

I was wearing dark trousers, my black Paul Smith jacket, a white shirt and proper shoes instead of trainers.

Mrs Sinclair sighed. 'It's a pity you didn't bring a nice suit, Ben. I should have warned you.'

'I haven't got a nice suit,' I said cheerfully. 'This is as formal as I get.'

Mrs Sinclair's sleek black Audi was parked in the drive.

'All right, you two, you can sit in the back,' she said. We all got in, and she drove us quickly through the winding Cornish lanes.

'Did you rent the house because this bloke Daumier is your client?' I asked.

There was a slightly embarrassed silence. Then she said, 'I didn't exactly rent it, it's on loan. Mr Daumier was very keen I should come down here to work on this trust business. He threw in the house as a sort of bonus. It was his family home until he moved to a newer house in Polzod, now he rents it out.'

Cassie frowned. 'Is that sort of thing strictly ethical?'

'Perfectly,' said her mother. 'Mr Daumier positively insisted I use the house, rent-free, for as long as I like. I wanted us to have a holiday, so the offer seemed too good to refuse.'

There was definite satisfaction in her voice. One of the reasons the rich stay rich is because they've got a keen eye for a bargain.

If you can call the free loan of a haunted house a bargain . . .

Thinking of the ghost reminded me of my earlier conversation with Cassie. The ghost was linked to the house, the house was connected to the murders – and the house had once been Mr Daumier's family home.

Maybe Cassie was right and Squire Daumier was our man.

If so, we were going to dinner in the lion's den.

I sat back, thinking hard.

Suppose, just suppose, Daumier was our unknown bigwig, the one who'd set the thugs on us. He wasn't likely to harm us in front of Cassie's mother. Not unless he was raving mad – which he might be, of course. If he was our man, he'd reacted pretty violently to our simple enquiry about the newspaper files for 1951 – which suggested he might be paranoid on the subject.

I might be worrying about nothing, he might not be

our man at all. All the same, I decided, it wouldn't hurt to take a few precautions.

'Mrs Sinclair, Cassie?' I said.

They both reacted to the urgency in my voice, and said, 'What?' more or less together.

'I want you to do something for me – and I don't want you to ask any questions, not right now anyway.'

'Go on,' said Mrs Sinclair cautiously.

I turned to Cassie. 'If, and only if, I say something about your school project, I want you and your mother to have a certain conversation . . . And speak up, so everybody hears it!'

I told them what I wanted them to say, and made them repeat it until I was sure they'd got it off pat. It didn't take long. Mrs Sinclair was a trained lawyer, used to memorising masses of material, and Cassie was a naturally quick study.

When I'd finished Cassie said, 'Brilliant, Ben!'

Mrs Sinclair said, 'What's going on? What are you two up to?'

'Tell you later,' I said.

She'd have asked more questions, but by now we were driving up the hill behind Polzod, towards a brilliantly illuminated white mansion.

I wondered what was waiting for us inside.

CHAPTER FOUR

THE SQUIRE

Squire Daumier lived in a modern mansion on top of the hill behind Polzod. It had fancy electronically operated wrought-iron gates, a circular carriage-drive, and a flight of steps leading up to a roofed portico, with white columns on either side.

The squire was standing at the top of the steps when we arrived. He was gazing down at the little town spread out below with an air of lordly satisfaction – natural enough, really, since he owned most of it.

He was a tall, handsome man of about sixty-something, with a tanned face, white hair, and a beaky nose. He was wearing polished brown brogues, cavalry-twill trousers, a beautifully-cut tweed sports jacket and a checked shirt with a silk scarf at the throat. He looked like a character from an old British film – or somebody modelling the complete country gentleman's outfit in a menswear catalogue.

Everything a bit too good to be true.

He watched while Mrs Sinclair parked the car in the driveway and we all got out. He stood waiting, posing really, as we climbed the steps towards him.

He greeted Mrs Sinclair with the sort of air-kissing that always irritates me, then turned to us with the kind of patronising smile that annoys me even more. The smile of someone who thinks that elder always means better.

'This is my daughter Cassandra,' said Mrs Sinclair. 'And her friend Ben Harker.'

Daumier looked from one to the other of us – and suddenly his smile turned into an astonished stare.

Mrs Sinclair gave him a puzzled look and he pulled himself together.

'How d'you do,' he said abruptly. 'Pleased to meet you.' He turned and led the way into the house.

I looked at Cassie and saw that, as so often happened, she knew what I was thinking. Daumier had recognised our descriptions – the descriptions given to him on the telephone by that man at the newspaper or the old lady in the library. He'd been fooled by the different clothes for a moment, but the penny had soon dropped. A lanky young man and a slim green-eyed young woman. He knew who we were all right. The question now was, what was he going to do about it?

He led us into the house, through an elaborately decorated foyer, and into a big, luxuriously-furnished sitting-room.

A small, tubby, balding man in gold-rimmed glasses was waiting to meet us. He looked like an anxious Mr Pickwick. Daumier waved a casual hand towards him. 'This is my cousin Henry, he helps with the business. Don't just stand there, Henry. Drinks!'

Henry jumped and hurried over to a drinks trolley. After a certain amount of bumbling about, he produced sherry for Mrs Sinclair and the Squire and lime juice for me and Cassie.

The Squire ignored him after that, except for waving his glass impatiently at him when he wanted a refill, which was often. He ignored us too, engaging Mrs Sinclair in a one-sided conversation, talking at rather than to her. He delivered a rambling monologue about how things had all gone to pot since the good old days, and the problems caused by lazy workmen and crippling taxation.

He varied this from time to time with accounts of all the important people he was on friendly terms with, and his own importance in the Polzod community. Then he moved on to a monologue about the stupidity of the family trust which stopped him selling the old house and developing his land.

Mrs Sinclair coped brilliantly, saying, 'Yes, indeed', 'How true', and 'Fascinating!' whenever there was a suitable gap.

Cassie and I, meanwhile, tried to make conversation with Cousin Henry, which wasn't easy. He was desperately shy, and terrified of his cousin Richard.

He brightened when I said how kind it was of them to lend us the old house.

'Do you like it? Richard and I grew up there, you know. Our fathers were brothers. I was always very happy there.'

'Why did you move?' asked Cassie.

'Oh, Richard said it was old-fashioned and inconvenient – which it was, I suppose. He wanted somewhere more up-to-date, more in keeping with his position. And there were unhappy memories, family memories . . .'

'Really,' said Cassie. 'How fascinating. Do tell us about it.'

Henry blossomed under her fascinated interest.

'Well,' he began, and for one wonderful moment I thought he was going to tell us all we wanted to know.

Then a thin old voice said, 'I hope you're not boring these young people with our tiresome family history, Henry.'

'Ah, Cousin Lavinia,' said Henry.

We turned and saw the white-haired old lady from the library.

We stared at each other in mutual astonishment.

Then Lavinia raised her voice. 'Cousin Richard, what an extraordinary coincidence. These are the two young people I was telling you about. The ones I was sadly unable to help with their researches – *into the year 1951.*'

Richard Daumier swung round in alarm. It was odd, I thought. He'd already realised who we were. He must be reacting to her mention of the actual date.

It was the perfect opportunity. I turned to Cassie. 'Don't start going on about that *school project* of yours,' I said loudly. 'You've been grumbling about it for ages; I'm thoroughly fed up with it.'

I looked hard at Mrs Sinclair, who recognised her cue and played up splendidly. 'It really is absurd,' she said to Richard Daumier. 'I just don't understand modern teaching methods.'

'What is this project?' asked Cousin Lavinia. Once again, there was a hard edge of curiosity to the sweet-old-lady voice.

'All Cassie's history class were given a year, and told

to research something that happened in it. No choice, the years were just handed out. What was yours, darling?'

'1951,' said Cassie gloomily. 'I mean, what a nothing year! As far as I can discover, absolutely nothing happened apart from the Festival of Britain, and who cares about that? I even thought of doing the project down here, in case there was some interesting piece of local history.' She looked at Lavinia and shrugged. 'But that didn't work out so . . .'

'Do you intend to continue your researches, my dear?' asked Cousin Lavinia. 'I checked with our local historian and he says he'll need the files for some time.'

Cassie shook her head. 'I can't be bothered. I'll fudge something up when I get home, something about the City of London. They'll like that.'

'Besides, it upsets the locals,' I said. 'Believe it or not, some local yobs told us to stop raking up the past and clear off. Quite nasty, they were!'

'When did this happen?' demanded Cassie's mother. 'Why didn't you tell me?'

'Oh, it was nothing,' I said evasively. I looked innocently at Cousin Lavinia. 'I can't think how they even found out what we were doing.'

'Oh dear, I'm afraid that may be my fault,' she said sweetly. 'It's quite possible I told someone who told someone else who told someone else.'

'News travels quickly in a small town,' said Richard Daumier. 'Gets exaggerated every time it's passed on. Probably thought you were journalists.'

I looked at him in surprise. 'At our age? Besides, why should it upset them so much?'

Daumier looked stumped, and turned appealingly to his cousin Lavinia.

'We had rather a sordid sex-murder here not long ago,' said Cousin Lavinia in shocked tones. 'A lot of tabloid journalists came down and had a field day. The local people felt it was smearing the name of their town; they became very sensitive on the subject. If they got the idea you were raking up more old scandal they would naturally resent it.'

It was a pretty thin story, I thought. But so was the story we were telling them. I wondered exactly who was fooling who.

Soon after that, thank goodness, it was time to go. Cassie and her mother excused themselves to visit the ladies' room.

Alone with the Daumiers, I had a sudden bright idea.

'It's very good of you to lend Mrs Sinclair the house, Mr Daumier,' I said. 'And of course it's better for you. With Cassie under her eye she'll be able to work properly.'

Richard Daumier looked baffled. 'Don't follow you.'

I explained that while Mrs Sinclair was a brilliant lawyer, she worried obsessively about her daughter.

'Once Cassie went missing for a few hours – nothing happened, she'd just gone off with some friends. Mrs Sinclair was so upset she couldn't work properly for weeks. She even worries about me because I'm Cassie's best friend. With both of us down here with her, enjoying a nice holiday, she'll do a much better job of breaking that family trust. If anything happened to us, she'd be useless to you.'

And I can't spell it out any plainer than that, I thought.

Richard Daumier looked thoughtfully at me. 'See what you mean . . .'

I'd used a similar tactic before, with a Russian Mafia thug called Lukas, who'd also believed he needed Mrs Sinclair's help. It had worked, too – for a time.

Cassie and her mother returned and we took our leave.

'Richard Daumier must be one of the biggest bores in the world,' said Mrs Sinclair as she drove us away. 'And believe me, I've met some in my time.'

'So why go for drinks with him?' asked Cassie.

Her mother looked surprised. 'Because he's a *client*.

52

Sorry to inflict him on you two though. Tell you what, there's a famous fish restaurant in the next town, we'll go out for dinner.'

We left Polzod and drove along the coastal road.

The famous fish restaurant overlooked the harbour in the picturesque little town of Tredstow. It was incredibly posh and amazingly expensive and the food was wonderful.

I'd hoped the distraction of the meal would take Mrs Sinclair's mind off earlier events, but she was just biding her time.

When the desserts had been cleared away and the coffee served she said, 'And now, you two, I want to know what you're up to. Exactly what's been going on?'

Cassie looked appealingly at me. I was the acknowledged spin-doctor of the partnership. I drew a deep breath and told Cassie's mother what had been going on. Not *exactly* though. I gave her an edited version.

For a start, I left out the bit about Cassie seeing the ghost, both in the house and on the cliffs at Maiden's Leap. But I told her about meeting the old man, and about his tale of a sensational suicide in Polzod. Not wanting to bring in the ghost, I said the old man had hinted the suicide was mixed up with a murder. I told her we'd worked out it must have happened in 1951 and decided to look it up, just to pass the time.

I told her about our visit to the newspaper office, the missing 1951 file and Mr Trefusis's strange over-reaction. I told her about Cousin Lavinia's odd reaction at the library. Finally I told her of the three threatening local yobs, leaving out all the actual violence – including Cassie's straight right!

When I'd finished she said flatly, 'It's incredible. Are you trying to tell me Richard Daumier sent people to threaten you just because you asked about a particular *year*?'

'Somebody did,' said Cassie. 'If it was him, he must be totally paranoid about it. That story about outraged citizens was rubbish. Those three couldn't have cared less about the fair name of Polzod.'

'I can see how he managed to get rid of the library file,' I said. 'He had Cousin Lavinia to sort that out. But how did he manage to erase the file on the newspaper's computer?'

'I may have the answer to that,' said Mrs Sinclair reluctantly. 'He owns the newspaper. I saw it on the list of his properties.'

'So he could do what he liked,' said Cassie. 'He got rid of the file and left orders to check up on anyone enquiring about local events in 1951.'

'Why on earth would he bother to go to such lengths?' demanded Cassie's mother.

'Let's say the murder happened in his house,' I said. 'The one we're living in now. In his house, and in his family. For some reason he lives in dread of somebody raking it up again.'

'But why?' insisted Mrs Sinclair. 'He's hardly likely to have been involved.'

'How old is he?' asked Cassie.

Mrs Sinclair thought for a moment. 'Richard? Somewhere in his sixties, I think. He'd still have been a teenager in 1951.'

I did a quick bit of mental arithmetic. 'He could have been fifteen or sixteen, even seventeen,' I said. 'There have been younger killers than that!'

'Perhaps it wasn't Richard at all,' said Cassie. 'Maybe it was his father or one of his uncles. Perhaps he's just worried about the disgrace to the family name.'

'It's true he's a terrible snob,' said Mrs Sinclair thoughtfully. 'Always going on about his "position" in the town. The locals call him the Squire as a joke, but he takes it all seriously.' She looked hard at me. 'So that was the point of that charade you made me go through – to convince him your interest in 1951 was sheer coincidence?'

I nodded.

'Will he believe it?'

'He might,' said Cassie. 'If only because he'll want to believe it.'

'I tried something else as well,' I said.

I told her the tale I'd spun when she and Cassie were out of the room.

'Terrific,' Mrs Sinclair said bitterly. 'That will do my professional reputation a lot of good.'

'All in a good cause,' I said. 'While he needs you, he won't bother us. You might twitch a bit next time you see him, just to make it more convincing.'

She gave me a look. 'Thanks a lot! It would be nice if every time I got a good client you two didn't discover he was a criminal or a madman – or both!'

I grinned. 'We'll try not to make a habit of it.'

'Be fair, Mum,' said Cassie. 'We saved your bacon over Lukas, remember.'

Lukas was the City wheeler-dealer Mrs Sinclair had got mixed up with.

Cassie's instincts had told her Lukas was a murderous criminal. He'd turned out to be a money-launderer for the Russian Mafia.

Mrs Sinclair smiled ruefully, summoned a waiter, paid the enormous bill without blinking and drove us home.

Back in the house she said, 'I'm off to bed. Don't stay up too late, you two.'

Cassie and I made some hot chocolate, sat chatting for a bit, and soon found we were yawning too. All the same, we were neither of us keen to go to bed.

There was still the ghost . . .

'Want to sit up all night?' I suggested. 'Or we could sleep in the sitting-room. You take the couch and I'll kip in the armchair.'

Cassie thought about it for a moment, then shook her head.

'I'm asleep on my feet,' she said. 'Besides, now we're helping the ghost it might calm her down a bit.'

We went off to bed.

Back in my room I switched on the laptop, logged on to the Internet and looked up 'Cornwall' and 'crime'. I got a lot of stuff about smugglers and Cornish wreckers, and accounts of some gruesome nineteenth-century murders – but there was nothing about a suicide and a murder in Fifties Polzod.

I switched off the laptop and went to bed.

A few hours later, I was woken by the sound of a scream coming from Cassie's room. I jumped out of bed, raced along the corridor and burst into her bedroom.

Cassie was sitting up in bed, her face twisted with terror.

Leaning over her was a glowing white apparition, its bony hands reaching for her throat . . .

CHAPTER FIVE

GHOST

I could see the apparition quite clearly this time. It was a girl, a scrawny-looking girl with lank black hair. She wore a long white cotton nightgown, and her thin face was twisted with hatred. The figure was almost, but not quite, transparent: there and not there at the same time.

The strange thing was that I wasn't frightened. I was just plain angry.

'Hey, stop that!' I yelled. 'Leave her alone!'

The ghost froze. Maybe it wasn't used to having its haunting interrupted.

I marched towards it, still angry. 'Listen, you stupid spook!' I shouted. 'We're trying to help you. We believe you're innocent. We're trying to find out what's supposed to have happened and what really did happen. We've already been in danger because of you. How can Cassie help you if you keep trying to strangle her or lure her over cliffs? She's no use to you dead, is she? Clear off and leave us alone. Don't come back unless you can be of some help.'

Slowly the ghost faded away.

I went over to Cassie, who was still trembling, sat on the side of her bed and put an arm around her shoulders. 'You all right?'

'More or less. That was some exorcism!'

'Well, honestly,' I grumbled. 'We knock ourselves out trying to help, and all it can do is pop up and try to kill you. Even a ghost should have more sense than that.'

'She's had a hard time,' said Cassie. 'Accused of murder, then murdered herself. No wonder she's a bit bitter and twisted –'

Suddenly Cassie's eyes widened and she stared over my shoulder. I turned and saw another white shape in the doorway.

It wasn't a ghost, this time. It was Cassie's mother in a white bathrobe.

'What's the matter, Cassie? I thought I heard you scream.'

'It's all right, Mrs Sinclair,' I said quickly, standing

up. 'Cassie had a nightmare, I heard her call out too.'

Mrs Sinclair ran over to Cassie and hugged her. 'Are you all right? Do you want to come and sleep in my room?'

'No, I'm fine now, Mum. Ben chased the nightmare away.'

'You're sure?'

'Yes, I'll be all right.'

Mrs Sinclair turned to me. 'I think I'll have a cup of tea in the kitchen now I'm up. Will you join me, Ben?' It was an order, not a request. She wasn't taking any chances!

'Be right with you,' I said.

She nodded, kissed Cassie goodnight and went out of the room.

I went over to Cassie and gave her a goodnight hug. She buried her head on my shoulder, and I could feel her shaking. For a moment I thought she was crying. Then I realised she was laughing!

She looked up at me, wiping her eyes. 'You certainly saw off that ghost! You don't stand any nonsense, do you, Ben?'

She gave me a quick kiss and my heart started pounding. I kissed her back and she responded for a moment and then pulled away. 'You'd better go and see Mum. I'm all right now.'

I made an attempt to be casual. 'Give me a shout if the ghost comes back.'

'I don't think it would dare!'

I went back to my room, grabbed a dressing-gown and went down to the kitchen, where I found Mrs Sinclair making tea.

'What's upsetting Cassie so much that she's having nightmares?' she asked.

I decided, not for the first time, to tell her a partial version of the truth.

'You know how sensitive Cassie is?'

It was as near as I could come to a reference to Cassie's psychic powers, a subject Mrs Sinclair found disturbing.

Mrs Sinclair nodded.

'She's got the idea that this house is haunted,' I went on. 'She thinks that the haunting is connected to whatever happened here back in 1951. That's why she's been having nightmares. And if you find me in her room at strange hours of the night, that's why.'

Mrs Sinclair looked worried. 'Do you think we ought to go home?'

'What about your Daumier deal?'

'The deal's important, but it's not as important as Cassie. Should we go?'

'I don't think so. She's kind of obsessed with the

mystery – we both are. I think it will be better for her if we stay here and solve it.'

Mrs Sinclair looked even more worried. 'Won't that be dangerous? You said you were threatened.'

'I hope not. As long as Daumier believes that if he needs your help he's got to leave us alone . . .' I paused. 'What are his chances of breaking this family trust?'

'Not bad. Mind you, courts are often reluctant to change that sort of thing without good reason. But if we can make a case that something set up sixty-odd years ago just isn't reasonable today . . .'

'Who set up the trust in the first place?'

'His grandfather. Apparently he didn't trust his eldest son, Richard's uncle Simon. It seems Simon was a bit of a black sheep, a spendthrift, and the old man was afraid he'd fritter away the family fortune. He couldn't stop Simon inheriting, but he tied up this house and the cliff-top land so they couldn't be sold.'

'What happened to the wicked Simon?'

'He died, and Peter, Richard's father inherited. He died a few years later, and Richard inherited from him, when he was still quite young.' She looked at her watch. 'I'd better get off to bed. I've got a meeting with Richard Daumier at his house tomorrow and I still haven't finished all my paperwork.'

She got up to leave, and paused in the doorway. 'You will take care of Cassie tomorrow, won't you, Ben? Find some nice harmless holiday things to do. Go and build sandcastles on Doombar Beach.'

'I'll try,' I said. 'We've got a busy day planned.'

But I was crossing my fingers behind my back. Cassie wasn't going to give up this investigation until she found some answers – and neither was I.

Next morning, after breakfast, Mrs Sinclair went off to prepare for her meeting, and Cassie turned to me with a determined look in her eye.

'Still stuffing yourself? Come on, lazybones, we've got work to do. We're searching the house today, remember?'

I hate it when she gets all brisk and efficient like that. I'm not really a morning person.

'All right, all right,' I grumbled.

I finished the last of my toast and swallowed my coffee. We stacked the breakfast dishes in the sink – a woman from the village came in twice a day and 'did' for us – and began our search.

We started in the attic, which held only empty packing cases, a few bits of broken furniture, and a box of broken toys. I tried to imagine little Richard and little Henry, playing with them years ago.

We searched the old house room by room, looking in drawers and cupboards, anywhere that might hold papers, or any other scrap of information.

We didn't find a thing – at least nothing that told us anything. The house held only the sort of thing you'd find in any holiday house. An assortment of old-fashioned furniture and faded carpets and curtains. Blankets and sheets and old-fashioned eiderdowns stowed away in store cupboards. A few old books and magazines left by earlier tenants.

We searched all the bedrooms, including our own, then went downstairs and did the kitchen and the ground-floor sitting-rooms. We even disturbed Mrs Sinclair in the study and searched shelves and cupboards and the old-fashioned roll-top desk she was working at. Nothing. Not a scrap of paper left from the days when the house was the Daumier family home.

'It's like the mysterious incident of the dog in the night-time,' I said, when we broke off the search for a cup of tea.

Cassie was tired and a bit cross by now. Our fruitless search was getting her down – even though, as I reminded her, it was all her idea.

'What are you on about now, Ben?'

'I can see you're no Sherlock Holmes fan,' I said. 'It's in a story called *Silver Blaze* about a stolen racehorse. There was a watchdog around at the time, but it gave no warning.'

'So?' said Cassie impatiently. 'Get to the point!'

'Well, old Sherlock remarks on "the curious incident of the dog in the night-time". The baffled cop points out that the dog did nothing in the night-time. "That," says Holmes, "was the curious incident!" '

Cassie looked puzzled for a moment – but only for a moment.

'The watchdog didn't bark when the horse was stolen – which meant that the thief was somebody the dog already knew.'

'Elementary, my dear Watson!'

'What's that got to do with us?'

'This house was the Daumier family home for generations,' I said. 'You'd think they'd have left *some* trace of themselves. It's as if the whole place has been stripped clean of every piece of paper, every scrap of information. I think the way we didn't find anything tells us something.'

'All it tells us is that Richard Daumier has something to hide,' said Cassie. 'And we knew that already!' She finished her tea. 'Come on, let's do the cellars. It's our last hope.'

You reached the cellar by opening a wooden door

on the other side of the kitchen. A flight of stone steps led downwards. I switched on the light, a bare bulb dangling from the ceiling by a length of flex, and we went down into the darkness beyond. There was another light-switch at the bottom of the stairs, and another dangling bulb lit up the dusty cellar.

I looked around. Stone walls, stone-flagged floor, whitewashed ceiling. The atmosphere was cold and dank.

From our point of view the place was a dead loss, empty except for rows of empty wine-racks lining the walls. They certainly hadn't left any booze behind.

I turned to Cassie. 'There's nothing here, we might as well –' I broke off.

Cassie was staring into space in a kind of trance.

'Cassie, what's up?'

She pointed and, after a moment, I saw it too.

A faintly-glowing white-robed figure stood on the other side of the cellar by one of the empty wine-racks. It became more distinct and I saw the same scrawny lank-haired figure we'd seen last night in Cassie's room.

For a moment we all stood there, frozen, motionless.

The figure pointed downwards and then faded slowly away.

After a moment we crossed the cellar and looked

where the apparition had pointed. A crumpled piece of newspaper lay on the cellar floor behind one of the wine-racks.

Cassie bent down and picked it up.

She carried it to the light and unfolded it carefully. It was torn from the front page of a local paper, the *Polzod Bugle* whose files we'd failed to find.

The date was October 12ᵗʰ 1956.

The headline read: *DOOMBAR RESIDENT DIES IN TRAGIC SHIPWRECK*

There was a sub-head: *Death in Sight of Home*

And a line of text: *Mr Peter Daumier, of Doombar House, perished –*

And that was all. The ragged tear cut across the rest of the article.

I looked at Cassie. 'It looks like our ghost decided to be helpful after all!'

CHAPTER SIX

SHIPWRECK

'Not *very* helpful,' I said, as we climbed the cellar stairs and went back into the sunlit kitchen. We got ourselves some lemonade. While we were drinking it, I studied the piece of newspaper again. 'Peter Daumier, Richard's father, died in a shipwreck. So what? What does it *mean*?'

'The ghost thinks it's important,' said Cassie. 'So it must mean *something*. It adds another piece to the jigsaw puzzle.'

'That's all very well,' I grumbled. 'The trouble with this jigsaw is, we haven't got the box with the picture on the lid!'

'We've just got to find out *more*,' said Cassie. 'More

about the murders, more about the shipwreck.'

I nodded. 'Daumier may have got rid of all the records here, but there must be some others somewhere. Other local papers maybe – he can't own all of them. If it was a sufficiently juicy murder it might even have made the nationals. And as for the shipwreck – aha!'

'Aha what?'

'Fancy another nice healthy walk to Polzod?'

'What for?'

'There's quite a decent-looking second-hand book-shop in one of the back streets – I noticed it yesterday. I bet it's got a local history section.'

Cassie looked worried. 'Suppose we meet those yobs again – the ones who threatened us?'

'It'll be an interesting experiment,' I said. 'If my plan last night works, Daumier will have told them to leave us alone – he won't want to upset your mother.'

'And if he didn't tell them, what do we do then?'

'Run like hell!'

We called in on Mrs Sinclair, who was surrounded with legal documents and textbooks in her study, and told her we were going into Polzod and would be back for supper.

'Stay out of trouble,' she said.

'I'll try.' I paused. 'Will you do me a favour?'

'If I can,' she said cautiously.

'When you see Daumier, find out his exact date of birth, and the dates when his Uncle Simon and Peter, his father, died. Tell him you need the information for legal purposes.'

'That's easy enough. I do need it as a matter of fact.'

'See if you can find out anything about *how* they died as well,' I added. 'Don't push that last bit though, we don't want him getting all suspicious again. Just a casual enquiry.'

Mrs Sinclair promised to do her best. Soon afterwards, Cassie and I set off. The walk along the cliff-tops was just as pleasant as it had been the day before – even better, since we stayed well clear of Maiden's Leap, and Cassie didn't see any ghosts.

We walked down the steep path into town, and strolled along the curved road that fringed the beach. The surf was up, and the beach was crammed. The smell of hot dogs and fish and chips was stronger than ever.

We were just about to turn off into the town when three all-too-familiar figures came out of an amusement arcade and walked towards us.

I looked at Cassie. 'Our friends from yesterday.'

'What do we do?'

'Just keep walking, show no fear. Just like with savage dogs. Oh, and don't hit anyone until I tell you.'

The unsavoury trio had recognised us as well. They came walking towards us. When they were close they came to a halt, barring our way.

I saw that the leader's nose was a fiery red.

I walked right up to him. 'How's the old schnozzle?'

He growled and lifted a fist.

The tall skinhead put a hand on his arm, and whispered something in his ear.

Reluctantly the thug lowered his fist. 'Clear off. You're safe – for now. And don't hang around, or you might still get what's coming to you.' He glared at Cassie. 'Especially you!'

'I'd be careful if I were you,' I said. 'She's got a wicked left hook! Well, it's been nice chatting to you.'

I took Cassie's arm and we walked forward. Reluctantly they moved aside and let us pass.

As we walked on, Cassie grabbed my arm. 'Are you mad?'

'Me? Why?'

'Talking to them like that!'

'I was just testing my theory – and I was right. They've been warned off, told to leave us alone. Told by someone who scares them so much that they overcame their desire to thump us.'

By now we'd reached the amusement arcade they'd come out of, and I paused and looked upwards.

'Well, well, there's one little mystery solved.'

'What do you mean?'

I pointed to the peeling nameboard above the door. In squiggly gold letters were the words *Wonderland Amusements. R. Daumier, Proprietor.*

'Daumier owns this place as well,' I said.

'So?'

'For some reason, amusement arcades are well-known hang-outs for dodgy characters,' I said.

'How do you know?'

I grinned. 'I used to spend a lot of time in them myself when I was younger.'

'Those three don't look as if they'd be scared of Daumier.'

I looked inside the arcade. A few shifty-looking types were pounding the pin-tables, and grappling with the electronic games. In the middle of the noisy room stood a massive bald-headed man. His brawny tattooed arms were folded over his belly and a leather change-pouch hung from his straining belt like a kangaroo's pouch. He was glaring suspiciously at us from small, piggy eyes.

I nodded towards him. 'If that's their boss, they might be scared of him. And if Daumier's *his* boss . . .'

We turned right into the old town, and made for the bookshop.

It was a wonderful old place, a real traditional second-hand bookshop. There were cheap paperbacks and ancient battered hardbacks on trays outside. The long interior room was crammed with books, not only on the rows of shelves, but stacked up in every available space. The nameboard over the window read *Pelligrew's Bookshop*.

We went inside. There was a counter just to the right of the door and behind it stood a tall, beaky-nosed, white-haired old man.

'Mr Pelligrew?' asked Cassie.

'Yes indeed. How may I help you, young lady?'

'I was wondering if you had anything on shipwrecks, particularly local ones.'

'Well, it's possible,' he said dubiously. 'We have a local history section, over there in the far left corner, if you'd care to look.'

We went over to the corner and started looking. It was hopeless. There were plenty of books, but they all seemed to be about Cornish tin mines, famous gardens, eighteenth-century smugglers and so on.

I touched Cassie's arm and she turned around from the shelf she was searching. 'Any luck?'

I shook my head. 'There might be something here, but it could take us weeks to find it.'

'Maybe I could help,' said Cassie.

'How?'

'Have you got that piece of newspaper about the wreck?'

I took it from my pocket and handed it to her.

'I'll hold this and concentrate,' she said. 'Think about the shipwreck, about the death of Mr Daumier of Doombar House. Maybe I can sense if there's anything here that connects with it.'

'Are you sure?' I asked anxiously. 'I know you don't like using your gift.'

'You're the one who's always telling me it can be a blessing, not a curse. I'd like to try, Ben.'

She held the piece of old newspaper in two hands and closed her eyes.

Everything seemed very still for a long, long time.

I was just thinking that she'd failed, when a book slid from an upper shelf and hit me on the head.

I yelped and Cassie opened her eyes.

'Ben, are you all right? What happened?'

'I'm not sure – but something did!'

I picked up the book. It was a solid old-fashioned volume with a black cloth cover. I opened the book to the title page. It was called *Wrecks and Wreckers of the Cornish Coast*.

I turned to the list of chapter headings. Most of them concerned the usual eighteenth-century wreckers and pirates stuff. But the last chapter was called 'A Modern Tragedy. Shipwreck at Doombar Bay – Strange Death of Peter Daumier.'

I showed the contents page to Cassie, pointing out the last chapter. 'Well done, Cassie!' I said. 'You didn't have to drop it on my head though!'

Cassie looked shaken and a bit far away. This sort of thing always took it out of her.

'Sorry, I didn't mean to.'

I put an arm round her shoulders and gave her a hug. 'Never mind. We'd never have found it without you.'

I closed the book and we hurried to the counter.

Old Pelligrew blinked benignly at us. 'Did you find what you want?'

'Yes,' said Cassie. 'We found exactly what we want.'

He took the volume from me and examined it.

'Dear me, I had no idea this was in stock. It's quite rare, but not particularly valuable. Shall we say five pounds?'

'That's fine.' I fished a crumpled fiver from the back pocket of my jeans and handed it to him. He put the book in a paper bag and handed it to me.

We were about to leave when I suddenly realised something. We'd been so excited by our find that we'd lost sight of the real mystery, the murder and alleged suicide.

I turned back to Mr Pelligrew.

'Do you have anything on true crime?' I asked. 'Particularly anything with a local interest.'

Mr Pelligrew gave me a strange look. 'Now there I really can't help you, I'm afraid.'

'No demand for it?' asked Cassie.

'Quite the contrary!' He leaned forward confidentially. 'I have a local customer, a very big customer, who is absolutely fascinated by local crime. One might almost say obsessed. He bought up all my existing stock, such as it was, years ago. Now he has a standing order that anything on the subject that comes in is to be shown to nobody but put aside and reserved for him. Price no object.'

I thought about Cousin Lavinia from the library and her 'local historian'.

Cassie obviously had exactly the same thought.

'That's a bit extreme, isn't it?'

Mr Pelligrew shrugged. 'As I said, the man is obsessed.'

'We wouldn't be talking about Mr Daumier by any chance?' asked Cassie. 'Mr Richard Daumier?'

Mr Pelligrew looked surprised. 'That is correct. I daren't disobey him, you see, he's my landlord. He said if I let him down he'd triple my rent and put me out of business.'

We found a nice crowded café in the busiest part of town and ordered coffees. We sat side by side, so we could both read the last chapter of the book at the same time.

It was quite a tale.

The writer began by explaining how Doombar Bay got its name. From the outside it looked like the ideal harbour, a deep cove sheltered by cliffs. But the bay was treacherous. A long sandbar, the Doombar, ran right across the entrance. It could be crossed by small vessels, or even by quite large ones if the tide was very high. But if the tide was too low, or the vessel too large – or worse still, both – the unlucky ship was in danger of breaking its back on the Doombar.

Once that happened, the ship was lost. Fierce tides would pound it up and down on the sandbar, or smash it to pieces on the nearby rocks.

In the eighteenth century, Cornish wreckers shone lights from the cliffs to lure ships on to the Doombar, so they could loot the cargo. Through the nineteenth century however, the dangers of the Doombar became more and more well-known. It was marked on all the charts and warning buoys were posted. Shipwrecks became fewer and fewer, and finally ceased altogether.

Then, in 1956, came the last and strangest wreck of all.

Mr Peter Daumier, a wealthy local businessman, was returning from a trip to France in his private steam-yacht, Nemesis. Astonishingly, he dismissed his two-man crew in Calais, instructing them to go home by ferryboat.

'I intend,' he said, 'to make my final voyage alone.'

Nemesis set sail, and was next sighted just off Doombar Bay. According to the harbourmaster, Mr Daumier was an experienced sailor who must have known that the tide was too low and the wind and waves too high for him to cross the Doombar in safety. Warning flares were fired, but he ignored them.

Nemesis sailed straight on to the Doombar, breaking her back. The skeleton of the wreck can be seen on the Doombar to this day. Mr Daumier's dead body was washed to shore several days later.

Speculation was rife as to the cause of Mr Daumier's inexplicable behaviour. There were rumours of deliberate suicide, but a charitable local coroner's jury brought in a verdict of accidental death.

Mr Daumier's son Richard, who inherited at age eighteen his father's business interests, said his father had been depressed since the tragic death of his elder brother Simon some years before . . .

There was quite a lot more, but it was mostly speculation and waffle.

To this day, the chapter ended, *the shattered wreck of the* Nemesis *still rests on the Doombar, clearly visible at low tide. A warning to other rash mariners, a tragic memorial to an inexplicable death and, ironically, an attraction for morbidly curious tourists.*

We closed the book and looked at each other.

'Suicide, quite definitely suicide,' said Cassie slowly.

I nodded. 'Five years after Simon's death. So if Peter killed Simon, brooded over it for five years and then committed suicide . . . maybe that accounts for Richard's behaviour. Nobody wants people to know his father was a murderer.'

'People *don't* know,' pointed out Cassie. 'We still don't know the details – but it seems likely that the verdict on Simon's death was murder, followed by the suicide of the girl who was supposed to have killed him – our ghost.' She gazed into space for a moment, then made one of her sudden leaps of intuition. 'You know what I think? I think proof still exists some-where. Proof that Peter killed Simon, proof that the girl's death wasn't really suicide, proof, maybe, that Richard was involved. Richard knows it exists, but he doesn't know where it is – and he's desperately afraid someone else will find it before he does!'

CHAPTER SEVEN

SCOOP

I couldn't help feeling that Cassie's ideas were pretty far-fetched. But before I could say so, we were interrupted. A young man came up to our table, carrying a cup of coffee.

'Join you?'

Without waiting for a reply, he pulled up a chair and sat down.

I looked around the café. It was busy, but there were still one or two free tables – tables he could have had to himself.

I waved towards the empty tables and said, 'Why?'

'Need to talk to you,' he said, in the same abrupt, jerky way.

I looked at him hard. With Daumier's thugs around, I was still a bit paranoid about strangers. He wasn't much older than I was, twenty if that, with black curly hair and blue eyes. Despite the heat, he wore a trenchcoat, hanging open over a blue denim shirt and black jeans.

I turned to Cassie. She was staring intently at the newcomer as if somehow absorbing him.

Suddenly she smiled. 'It's all right, Ben. He's OK.'

The stranger grinned. 'Must have an honest face.'

'Not specially,' I said, and it was true. Despite his youth, there was something a bit flash, a bit knowing about him, and his face had an expression of cheerful cynicism. 'It's more that I trust her judgement.'

He gave Cassie an admiring smile. 'Don't blame you,' he said. 'Would myself.' He turned back to me. 'Don't mind my asking – is she your girlfriend?'

'Yes!' I said firmly, not too sure of Cassie's reaction. Hurriedly I changed the subject. 'What do you want to talk to us about?'

'Richard Daumier, our beloved local Squire.'

'Why?'

'Think you've got something on him.'

He produced a card from his top pocket and handed it over.

It read: *William Skeffington. Journalist. Polzod Pioneer.*

There was an address, phone number and e-mail address underneath.

'The local paper Daumier *doesn't* own,' I said.

He nodded. 'That's the one.'

Cassie looked at the card and then at the journalist.

'I bet they call you Scoop!'

He grinned. 'I like it! Scoop Skeffington! No, they don't call me that yet, but they will one day! Right now they just call me Skeff. And you two are?'

I looked again at Cassie and she nodded. We gave him our names and our holiday address. He produced a notebook and wrote it all down.

'So why come to us?' asked Cassie.

'Guy called Tubby Barker, runs the amusement arcade for Daumier, does all his dirty work. Story going round the pubs, Tubby sent three of his thugs to warn off a couple of kids – sorry, young people – matching your descriptions. Thugs came out of it badly. One of them got a bloody nose – from the girl! All the other low-lifes thought it was a riot. Next thing, Tubby gives orders, kids to be left strictly alone. So come on, what's the story?'

'Why are you so interested in Daumier?' I asked.

'Because I think he's a crook, and maybe a murderer as well.' He saw our astonished reaction and said, 'You too? Come on, give!'

'You first, Skeff,' said Cassie.

'Came here a couple of years ago,' he began. 'First job after journalism school, have to start in the sticks. Started looking round, soon found out Daumier runs the town. Owns a pile of properties, most of the businesses, has a share in lots of others.'

'So he's the local tycoon,' I said, playing devil's advocate. 'That doesn't make him a crook – or a murderer.'

'Found out something else. Anyone who gets in Daumier's way is in big trouble.'

'How do you mean?' I asked. 'Give us an example.'

'Nice young couple take over a rundown pub. Do it up – good food, good booze, nice atmosphere. Starts taking money away from Daumier's places.'

'What happened?'

'Gang of roughs start using the pub. Fights every night, place smashed up, customers start staying away. Young couple go bust, Daumier buys the pub cheap.'

'Any other stories like that?' asked Cassie,

'Dozens. Daumier owns the big boatyard. Little boatyard nearby, family business, better workmanship, lower prices. Mysterious fire one dark night, little boatyard burns down.'

I looked at Cassie. 'What did I tell you? The Godfather of Polzod.'

'What about the police?' she asked. 'Can't they do anything?'

Skeff shrugged. 'Squire Daumier plays golf with the Chief Superintendent, gives generously to police charities. Mind you, I daresay they'd have to act if there was solid evidence – but there isn't. Daumier always works through others, everyone's scared to talk.'

'Can't you expose him in your paper?' asked Cassie.

Again Skeff shook his head. 'Proprietor's too cautious, scared of being sued.'

'Who owns the *Pioneer* then?'

'Big London syndicate, runs dozens of local papers. Doesn't care about the community so long as the papers make a profit.'

'You called Daumier a murderer,' said Cassie. 'What's that all about?'

'About six months ago a journalist came down from the *News of the Screws*.' He saw Cassie's face and said, 'Sorry, trade nickname! Big national paper, specialises in crime, sex and scandal. Man called Sam Turner, real old Fleet Street hack. Had a few drinks with him, said he was researching a Famous Crimes of the Past series. Wouldn't say any more.'

'What happened to him?' I asked – although I had a nasty feeling I already knew the answer.

'Found at the bottom of the cliffs. Official story was, he got drunk and wandered over the edge.'

'And you think Daumier was responsible?'

'Sure of it. No proof, though.' He paused. 'I liked old Sam.'

'What makes you so sure it wasn't an accident?' asked Cassie gently.

'Old Sam hated the country and the open air, couldn't wait to get back to London. When they closed the pub, he staggered back to his hotel in the town. Last thing he'd do, go for a walk on the cliffs, drunk *or* sober.'

'I think you're right, Skeff,' I said. 'Researching into old crimes isn't healthy round here.'

'Right, your turn,' said Skeff eagerly. He looked like a terrier who'd got a sniff of a rabbit.

I looked at Cassie and she nodded. 'You tell him, Ben, you're the talker.'

I gave Skeff the edited version, the one I'd given Cassie's mother.

The one without the ghost.

I told him how we'd heard of the mysterious suicide at Maiden's Leap, and decided to look into it. I told him of the events at the *Polzod Bugle* and at the library and of our trouble with the three thugs. I told him about Cassie's mother working for Richard

Daumier, and about our meeting with him, and with Cousin Lavinia. Finally I told him how, quite by chance, we'd come across an account of Daumier's father's mysterious death in the shipwreck of the *Nemesis*.

Skeff listened in fascinated silence, scribbling the occasional note.

'All this will have to be off the record,' I warned him. 'We haven't any more proof than you have, and we don't want to be sued either.'

Or killed, I added mentally, though I kept the thought to myself.

'Don't worry,' said Skeff. 'Not a word till we get cast-iron proof. I want to survive as well!' He paused for a moment, studying his notebook. 'It all ties together, though. Old Sam was researching a crime of the past. Must be the one that got you two in trouble.' He slammed his notebook shut. 'So – first thing to do, find out what happened in 1951.'

'How?' asked Cassie. 'Will it be on file at your paper?'

'No chance. Only founded in the swinging Sixties.' He paused, considering. 'Can't help you there – but I know a man who can.'

'Who?'

'I've got a contact on the good old *Screws*. Man

called Kelly, came down here to see about Sam's funeral.'

'Are you sure they'll have the story on file.'

'Are you kidding? The *Screws* have covered every sordid and sexy crime there ever was – their speciality. Been doing it for years; they were founded in the Thirties.'

'Will they let you see the file?' I asked.

'Don't see why not. Professional courtesy. Besides, if I tell Kelly all this links up with Sam Turner's death, and might help to prove it was murder . . .' He jumped up, eyes shining with excitement. 'Boy, if I break this story it's my ticket to Fleet Street! I'll call Kelly right away, and ask him to e-mail me the file. Should get a reply tomorrow, maybe even today if he gets a move on. Either of you two got a laptop?'

'I have,' I said.

'Give me your e-mail address.'

I gave it to him and he copied it into his notebook.

'Right, as soon as I get the info, I'll e-mail it on to you. Call me at the *Pioneer* when you get it – still got my card? – and we'll meet to decide the next move.'

He strode out of the café like a whirlwind, coat-tails flying behind him.

'Quite a character,' I said.

Cassie nodded. 'I liked him.'

She caught the look on my face and grinned mischievously.

'It's nice to know I'm officially your girlfriend, Ben.'

I scowled at her. 'The last person who asked me that question was Jason. I came over all noble and tolerant – caused no end of trouble.' I stood up. 'Come on!'

'Where?'

'We can't do much until we hear from Skeff – and I'd like to get out of Polzod while the truce is still on. Let's go to Doombar Bay and spend the afternoon on the beach.'

We got out of Polzod unharmed. I was careful to choose a route that didn't lead past the amusement arcade. No point in pushing your luck.

We climbed the steep lane to the cliff-top, walked along the path to Doombar House, and carried on down the steep lane that led to the beach.

Doombar Bay was very different from the bay at Polzod. It was smaller, narrower across the entrance, and cut deeper into the cliffs. Looking out to sea, the left side was lined with grass-covered sand dunes. On the right the cliffs came right down to the beach. The sea had carved a series of little niches in the cliffs, giving the feeling of small private booths.

There's a small car park bordering the beach, and at

the back of the car park is the combined beach shop and snack bar. The shop sells buckets and spades, inflatable rubber mattresses and boats, wind-breaks, flip-flops – everything you could ever need on the beach.

The snack bar provides sweets, ice-cream, hot dogs, hamburgers, sandwiches and Cornish pasties.

We were both starving by now so we headed straight for the snack bar and bought two cans of Coke and an assortment of junk food for lunch.

Cassie bought some magazines, I bought a paperback thriller and we headed for the beach.

It wasn't high season yet, and we managed to find a vacant niche. We settled down with our backs to the cliff rock and scoffed up our food and drink. Cassie was still hungry so I slogged back to the beach shop for ice-creams.

How she eats so much and stays so skinny I'll never know.

We polished off the ice-cream and sat back, stuffed but happy, to watch the beach activity. Little groups were scattered on the sand: mums, dads, kids, dogs, all having a wonderful time. People were swimming, paddling, building sandcastles, flying kites. No surfers, thank goodness, apparently the Doombar waves weren't right.

The tide was coming in now, covering the Doombar and the wreck of the *Nemesis*. Both were exposed only at the lowest of low tides.

We tried to read for a bit, but the exercise – walking to Polzod and back – the food and the sun made us sleepy. Cassie dozed off first, her head on my shoulder. I put down my book and sat as still as I could so as not to wake her.

A perfect afternoon. Except . . .

I had the strangest feeling I was being watched. I turned my head suddenly and looked up. I thought I saw a shadowy figure duck back from the cliff-edge above us.

Had I imagined it? Or were we really being watched?

There didn't seem to be anything I could do about it, so I tried to put it out of my mind.

Eventually I dozed off as well.

We were both woken up, more or less at the same time, by the crashing of the waves. The sea, comfortably far away when we'd first arrived, was only metres away. Soon it would be lapping at our feet.

That was the trouble with the niches – the sea filled them up at high tide. Linger too long and you faced the choice of climbing an uncomfortably steep cliff, or swimming. Or drowning, of course . . .

Hurriedly we gathered up our possessions and our litter and ran for the car park, getting out of the niche just as the sea came in.

Back at Doombar House, we found Cassie's mother, just returned from a long conference with Richard Daumier. We got a glass of wine for her, and Cokes for us from the big old-fashioned fridge and took them into the sitting-room.

'How did it go?' I asked.

'Not too well. He was tetchy and a bit vague, found it hard to concentrate. I got those dates for you though.'

She fumbled in her briefcase and fished out a sheet of paper.

'Richard Daumier was born in 1933 – a fact he was most reluctant to admit.' She smiled. 'Vanity, I suppose, he's older than he looks.'

So he'd have been eighteen when his uncle died – quite old enough to have been involved in some way, I thought.

'His uncle Simon died in 1951,' she went on.

The same year as the Maiden's Leap suicide – if it was a suicide. The two events *must* be connected.

'His father Peter died five years later, in 1956.'

Which we already knew from our shipwreck book, but it didn't seem tactful to say so.

'I couldn't get him to say anything about *how* his uncle and his father died,' said Mrs Sinclair. 'All he would say was that both died in tragic circumstances. He said he didn't wish to revive painful memories. He was getting quite agitated, so I followed instructions and didn't persist. Any help?'

'Terrific!' I said.

'As a matter of fact, we know how his father died,' said Cassie. 'We found a book in a second-hand bookshop in Polzod. Where's the shipwreck book, Ben?'

I looked round and found it on a side table, with Cassie's magazines and my thriller.

I opened it at the last chapter and handed it to Cassie's mother.

She fished out her reading glasses and scanned the chapter. It only took her a few minutes.

'If I was working for his insurance company, I'd advise them not to pay!'

'What do you mean?' asked Cassie.

'Suicide,' said her mother, with a lawyer's expertise. 'Suicide without a doubt. Dismissing his crew and talking about "making his last voyage alone". Then sailing into a familiar harbour at a time when he *must* have known it was dangerous. The coroner's jury was just being tactful − either that, or some family influence was brought to bear. No wonder Richard didn't want to talk about it.' She paused, looking thoughtful. 'We still don't know how his uncle died earlier, in '51. He didn't want to talk about that either.' She paused, remembering. 'I got an odd feeling he was covering something up.'

'Why?' I asked.

'Call it lawyer's instinct. We get lied to a lot, and you learn to recognise the symptoms.'

Cassie looked at me, and I looked at my watch. How long would it take Skeff's friend Kelly to find the information and e-mail it to Skeff? If he was away, or very busy, or just not too bothered . . .

I wanted to go and check my e-mail but I made myself be patient.

Sooner or later we'd know the *official* story of the death of Simon Daumier and the apparent suicide of the unfortunate maid, and of the connection between them.

But how were we going to discover the real truth?

CHAPTER EIGHT

THE CRIME

Cassie's mother asked if we wanted to go out to eat. But we were both tired, and I could see she was too. They both offered, rather half-heartedly, to cook supper, but I said I'd do it. In fact I insisted.

'What's come over you?' said Cassie. 'Why are you being so helpful?'

'Partly to establish my credentials as a genuine New Man – but mostly it's self-protection. I've sampled your cooking before.'

I fled to the kitchen before they could react.

It was quite true what I'd said. Cassie's mother had never been the domestic type, and Cassie hadn't bothered to learn. As far as I could gather, they either ate out or lived on takeaways.

I, on the other hand, had been motherless since I was very young. To save myself from the efforts of a series of not-very-competent housekeepers, I'd been forced to learn how to cook a few simple dishes. I'd found I actually enjoyed it.

I rooted through the kitchen – Mrs Sinclair had laid in a few supplies – found the ingredients for my famous spaghetti carbonara and set to work.

After supper, which we ate at the kitchen table, Mrs Sinclair went off to mull over the information from the meeting, and Cassie and I piled the dishes in the sink and sat chatting.

'I feel sort of suspended,' said Cassie. 'We can't do anything till we get the newspaper stuff from Skeff's friend, and even then . . .'

'We may not be able to do anything anyway,' I concluded for her. 'Still, it would be nice to know.'

Cassie looked at me hopefully. 'Is it worth checking? I mean, the Internet can move at the speed of light . . .'

Cassie's a million times brighter than me about most things, but she's not really into computers. I'm the one with the laptop and the tekkie tendencies.

'It's a bit soon . . .' I said.

Her face fell.

'But there's no harm in checking.' I stood up, and Cassie started to get up as well. 'Stay here and I'll get the laptop from my bedroom,' I said. 'There's a phone socket and I can easily set up here.'

She sat down again and I went and collected the laptop and set it up on the kitchen table. I typed in my password and, after the usual maddening delay, logged on. Cassie looked on over my shoulder.

When the logging-on process was complete, the usual icon flashed up: *You've got e-mail.*

'It's here!' said Cassie excitedly.

I couldn't resist teasing her. 'Don't get your hopes up, it could be anybody. Could be Dad, could be one of my friends from school. We often send each other e-mails. Maybe it's Charlie or Yvonne . . .'

For some reason Cassie never liked my mentioning Yvonne.

'Get on with it, you Internet anorak!'

I opened the e-mail. It was from Skeff. We read it together.

Dead lucky, managed to get hold of old Kelly, impressed him with urgency. News of Screws dead keen to clear up Sam's death. Sent me the attached, which I'm passing on to you. It's sensational!

Call me at the Pioneer tomorrow a.m., all best,
Skeff.

I opened up the attachment.

It was a copy of a newspaper report:

BRUTAL SLAYING
OF PLAYBOY BUSINESSMAN

Passion and Murder Come to Peaceful Cornwall!

Suicide of Guilty Maid

*The picturesque seaside resort of Polzod was rocked
yesterday by the brutal slaying of one of the town's most
popular figures, sporting tycoon and racehorse owner, Mr
Simon Daumier.*

*The popular businessman, who had a wide circle of
friends, was found dead in his study by his brother, Mr
Peter Daumier, and his nephew Richard. His skull had
been completely shattered by a single blow from some
heavy blunt instrument.*

*The police were immediately summoned and the
domestic staff questioned. Soon it was discovered that one
of the under-maids was missing. Her name was Emily
Tregorran.*

We stopped reading and looked at each other. Our
ghost had a name: Emily. Emily Tregorran.

We read on.

Emily's room was searched and, almost immediately, a heavy brass candlestick, its base smeared with blood, was found. Wrapped around the candlestick was a scrawled semi-literate note:

'He done me wrong and wouldn't make it right. I was a good girl till I come to Doombar House. I begged him to marry me but he just laughed. He was drunk.

'He shoved me away and I grabbed the candlestick and hit him. I didn't mean to kill him, but I done it and I can't face the shame. I shall end it all.

Emily Tregorran.'

The bloody fingerprints on the note, and on the candlestick have been established as being those of Emily Tregorran,

The handwriting, although shaky, was identified by Mr Richard Daumier, the dead man's nephew, as identical to that on her letter of application for employment.

Mr Daumier said, 'My uncle was an honourable man and I'm sure that the girl's accusation is unfounded. I am convinced that the poor girl was deluded. She was always strange. My late uncle was a handsome man and very attractive to women. I am convinced that Emily formed an attachment to him, and convinced herself that they were lovers.'

As yet the unfortunate girl's body has not been found.

Attached to the main report was a shorter one, dated a few days later.

The body of Emily Tregorran, the housemaid who confessed to the recent murder of Mr Simon Daumier, was washed up last night in Doombar Bay. Much damaged by pounding against the rocks, the body was identifiable only by dental records.

In view of the state of the body, and the girl's clear confession, it was decided that, to spare the feelings of the girl's family, no autopsy was necessary. The body was released to the girl's parents for burial . . .

Just as we finished reading, Mrs Sinclair came in. She looked mildly surprised to see us huddled over the laptop.

'What are you two up to? Computer games?'

'Not exactly. We made friends with a local journalist and he managed to get us the newspaper report of Richard's uncle Simon's death. It's from a national newspaper.'

'Is it interesting?'

'Sensational!' I scrolled back to the beginning of the attachment and stood up. 'Take a look.'

Mrs Sinclair sat down in front of the laptop, and scrolled rapidly through the report. When she'd finished I said, 'What do you make of it – professionally?'

These days she worked mostly on corporation law, or on things like the business of breaking Richard Daumier's family trust. But I knew from Cassie that she'd done criminal law when she started at the bar – including several murder cases.

She skimmed rapidly through the report a second time before replying. Then she looked up and said, 'Fishy. Distinctly fishy.'

'Why?' asked Cassie eagerly.

'It's all much too pat – too neat and convenient. Notice how the only account of what happened comes from the Daumiers. And *Richard* does all the talking! Pretty cool for – what would he have been then?'

'Eighteen,' I said. 'Anything else?'

'There's the question of the extreme force of the blow – was Emily strong enough to shatter a man's skull? Then there are all the things that *didn't* happen.'

'Like the curious incident of the dog in the night-time,' I said.

Cassie gave me a look and asked, 'What sort of things?'

'The fact that no handwriting expert was called in, to verify that the note was really in the girl's handwriting. Richard vouched for it, for heaven's sake, and they just accepted his word. No autopsy to see if she was pregnant.' She stood up. 'If that girl had survived, and gone on trial, I'd have introduced enough element of doubt to get her off.'

'Can anything be done now – to clear her name, I mean?' asked Cassie.

'Not a chance, the case is closed. Mind you, if you had new evidence, substantial new evidence, something might be possible. But it still wouldn't be easy, not after fifty years.'

'We're seeing our journalist friend tomorrow,' I said. 'He may have more information. We'll let you know if he turns up anything useful.'

Mrs Sinclair went off to bed, and I logged off and shut down the laptop.

'Poor Emily,' said Cassie softly. 'Maybe we can still get her off.'

'I don't see how,' I said gloomily. I tapped the laptop. 'All we've got here is what's supposed to have happened. The official version. The only one who knows what really happened is Richard Daumier, and I don't think he'll tell us.'

'Someone else knows,' said Cassie.

'Who?'

'Emily – our ghost.'

'Maybe – but you never know when she'll turn up.'

'We could summon her,' said Cassie. 'Call her up.'

I looked anxiously at her. She was pale but determined.

'Are you sure, Cassie? I know how you hate doing that sort of thing.'

She smiled affectionately at me. 'Not as much as I used to – thanks to you, Ben. You were the one who taught me my – gift could be used in a good cause.'

I looked at her in surprise. This was a new, more confident Cassie.

'All right, Cassie. If you're sure.'

'We need to call up the ghost.'

'All right. What do we do?'

'We hold what the spiritualists call a *séance*. They turn out all the lights and sit in a circle holding hands.'

'The holding hands bit sounds good,' I said. 'Let's give it a go.'

I turned out the lights and then made my way back to the table.

Cassie and I sat on opposite sides of the table, leaning forward so each could hold both of the other's hands.

For a while nothing happened.

The room was almost completely dark, except for a faint glow of moonlight, coming through the window. I was feeling uneasy, and tried to cheer myself up.

'Didn't the spiritualists produce ghostly floating

drums – and tambourines? Can you rustle up a tambourine, Cassie?'

'Shut up, Ben,' said Cassie quietly. 'She's coming. She's very near. I can feel her . . .'

Cassie's green eyes were wide open, staring straight ahead, reflecting a faint gleam of moonlight.

A sort of electric quiver ran through Cassie's arms and the air grew cold.

Suddenly the ghost was there, standing by the door like a visitor unsure of her welcome.

Cassie let go of my hands and leaned towards her.

'Emily,' she said gently. 'Emily Tregorran.'

The ghostly form flickered for a moment and then became distinct again.

'We know who you are,' said Cassie. 'We know what they said about you, and we believe you're innocent. But you're the only one who knows what really happened – at least the only one who will tell us. You spoke before, can you speak again? Can you tell us what happened? Or show us?'

For a moment nothing happened.

Then I heard a thin ghostly voice inside my head. A girl's voice with a soft Cornish accent.

'It were late at night, and I were in bed. I heard shouting and I were frightened . . . I went down to see what was wrong . . .'

Suddenly the ghostly shape expanded into a white cloud, rushing towards us and swallowing us up . . .

I was somewhere else . . .

I was watching a thin, scrawny girl in a worn cotton nightgown creep barefoot down a long dark staircase towards the sound of raised voices.

She followed the turn of the staircase, and saw light blazing from the open doorway of a luxurious study. There were two men in the study and they were shouting angrily at each other.

One man was huge and fat with a face flushed with anger. He sat in a leather armchair, a tray of drinks at his elbow, and he was drunk.

The other man, standing over him, was short and thick-set, broad-shouldered and strong.

Somehow I knew that the fat man was Simon Daumier, the stocky one his brother Peter.

'You've ruined yourself,' Peter was shouting, 'and now you're ruining us! Business after business sold to pay for your slow horses and your losing bets and your champagne and your loose women. We'll all be paupers if this goes on. What about my future, and my son Richard's? What about Lavinia and little Henry?'

Fascinated and horrified, the girl moved closer to the door.

In a thick boozy voice, Simon said, 'Clear off, you

pompous little puritan. Don't know how to enjoy yourself, that's your problem.'

'Listen to me, damn you!' screamed Peter, and tried to drag his brother from his chair. Simon flung his drink in his face.

Wiping the burning spirit from his eyes, Peter staggered back, stumbling against an ornamental side-table holding two heavy brass candlesticks. Mad with rage, he snatched up one of the candlesticks, sprang forward, and brought the base of the candlestick smashing down on his brother's head.

The fat man's head seemed to explode.

The girl turned to run but someone came quickly up the stairs behind her, grabbed her arm with a strong hand and dragged her into the room. She turned and saw a tall young man. It was Peter's son, Richard.

The Richard Daumier of fifty years ago.

Peter himself was staring down at his brother's body, as if unable to believe what he had done.

'She saw it,' said Richard. 'She saw it all. She'll have to go.'

As the girl struggled to break free, he hit her hard under the jaw and she collapsed, unconscious.

Everything went black . . .

I was back at the kitchen table with Cassie and I was shaking all over. I looked towards the door and was relieved to see that the ghost had gone. I jumped up and put on the lights. Then I went back to the table, dragged a chair close to Cassie's and put my arms round her.

She was shaking too, and there were tears in her eyes. 'You saw it too?' she whispered.

I nodded. 'Some *séance*,' I said. 'I think I'd sooner have had a tambourine!'

'Well, we know what really happened now,' said Cassie. 'Peter killed Simon, Richard killed Emily, and then tidied it all up.'

I nodded. 'They wiped the top bit of the candle-stick, put Emily's prints on it, and put it in her room. They forged the suicide note, put Emily's prints on that too and left it with the candlestick for the cops to find. Then Richard threw Emily's body over the cliffs at Doombar Point.'

'What about the others in the house?' asked Cassie. 'Servants, family members . . . They must have had some idea.'

'Scared, or maybe bribed. I think mostly they just didn't want to know.'

Cassie nodded. 'Then Peter couldn't live with what he'd done and committed suicide by deliberately wrecking the *Nemesis* five years later. And Richard lived happily ever after.'

'Not if we've got anything to do with it,' I said grimly.

Cassie said, 'Yes, but have we? We know what really happened now – but what can we do about it, after fifty years?'

I didn't have the answer to that just yet, so I went and made us some cocoa.

Cocoa is very comforting in a crisis.

We talked a little longer and went to bed.

I lay awake for a while, trying to find a way to clear Emily's name and bring Richard Daumier to justice. I was still searching for the answer when I fell asleep . . .

CHAPTER NINE

MESSAGE FROM THE DEAD

I got a good night's sleep – which was something of a surprise, especially after that *séance*. I think I must have been psychically exhausted – all spooked out.

Next morning, Cassie said she'd slept well too – the ghost hadn't put in another appearance.

When breakfast was over, her mother had gone off to catch up on yet more paperwork and we'd stacked the dishes, Cassie sat me down at the kitchen table and said, 'Listen, Ben, I've had an idea.'

'Not another *séance*?'

'You remember how we were talking about why Richard Daumier was so paranoid about his past? And how nothing we'd found out could really harm him?'

I nodded. 'We could embarrass him, but that's about all. As your mother said, there's no new evidence.'

'And I said I thought some evidence must exist somewhere. Richard can't find it, but he's scared someone else will?'

'Hardly likely, is it? I mean, if he's been looking for fifty years . . .'

'I still think that evidence exists,' said Cassie. 'What's more, I've thought of a way to find it.'

'Go on.'

'You remember when Lukas kidnapped Mum and we didn't know where she was? And you persuaded me to use my locket as a pendulum, and swing it over a map to find her? Well, I've still got the locket!'

She pulled it up from inside her T-shirt, a locket on a thin gold chain.

I stared at her. 'And you want to use it to find the missing evidence? Is that possible? I mean, you had a perfectly clear memory of your mother. We don't even know what this evidence looks like – or even if it exists.'

'It's bound to be some kind of message: a letter, a notebook, a diary, something like that,' said Cassie confidently. 'If I concentrate on the subject and all we learned last night . . .'

'Well, no harm in trying,' I said.

I went into the study and collected a large scale map of Cornwall, telling Cassie's mother we were planning a trip.

I took it back to the kitchen, put it on the floor, and opened it.

'I'd start with the area around Polzod and Doombar Bay,' I said. 'I reckon if this evidence does exist, it's hidden somewhere local,' I said.

We sat cross-legged before the map and Cassie took off her locket. She began swinging it like a pendulum to and fro across the map. The locket swung wildly as if moved by some hidden energy.

'There's something there,' whispered Cassie. 'I can feel it. But I can't seem to focus, to narrow it down.'

The locket went on swinging wildly, and I began to think we were getting nowhere. Then, quite suddenly, it began swinging in narrower and narrower arcs.

Finally it settled over Doombar Bay.

I had a wild hope that the evidence might be in the house we were in, which would make life easier. No such luck. It began swinging in a dead straight line, over the Doombar itself.

Then it came to a dead halt over the centre of the bar.

Cassie looked up, her eyes shining. 'Of course – the

wreck. The evidence is on the wreck! Who more likely than Peter Daumier to write a confession? And where else would he leave it but on the *Nemesis*?'

'Don't you think Richard would have thought of that? I bet he searched that ship from top to bottom right after the shipwreck.'

'Maybe he did, but he didn't find anything. That evidence is still there and we're going to find it.'

'What makes you so sure?'

'The pendulum never lies!'

It was nice to see her so happy and confident – and a bit worrying as well.

'Listen,' I said. 'When I encouraged you not to be afraid of your powers, I didn't mean you to take up the paranormal for a hobby. You'll be flying about on a broomstick next!'

'I wonder if I could,' said Cassie thoughtfully. 'They used to rub some special magic ointment all over them, didn't they? I'll look up the ingredients when we get home.' She laughed at my worried look. 'Don't worry, Ben. I won't turn you into a frog unless *absolutely* necessary.'

She looked at my still-worried face and her smile disappeared. Suddenly she looked desperately unhappy.

'Ben, don't!'

'Don't what?'

'Don't start being afraid of me – like Jason.'

My friend Jason had a serious crush on Cassie – enough to worry me quite a bit. But when he'd discovered her psychic powers, and seen them in action, he'd backed off . . .

'It's only because of you I can do these things,' Cassie went on. 'You were the one who made me feel I wasn't a freak, stopped me from being afraid.' Her eyes filled with tears. 'Don't you go off me too, Ben, I need you!'

I was too choked up with emotion to speak. I leaned forward, grabbed her by the shoulders and kissed her hard and she kissed me back.

When I'd got my breath back I said, 'I wouldn't worry too much about me going off you, Cassie. It'll never happen.'

Cassie broke away, jumped up and grabbed the map. 'I'll take this back. There's something else I need.'

Pulling myself together, I called Skeff at the *Pioneer*. They said he hadn't come in yet. Either he'd overslept or he was out on an assignment. I left a message to call me and said I'd ring later.

Cassie came back clutching a sort of cardboard folder filled with dates and times.

'I found an up-to-date tide table.'

'So?'

'Well, it's spring tides. Today's almost the end of the springs. If it had been neaps we'd be done for.'

'Translation please!'

'There are two kinds of tides,' said Cassie patiently. 'Neaps, which mean low highs and high lows. And springs, which mean high highs and low lows.'

My head was starting to spin.

'Which means?'

'When it's low tide tonight, it will be *very* low. Which means we can almost walk out to the Doombar – and the wreck. We may have to swim the last bit, but it won't be far.'

'Hang on a minute – you want us to go out to the wreck?'

'Well of course. How else will we find what we're looking for?'

'So how do we get back?'

'If we judge things right, we'll have just enough time to search the wreck. Then the tide will turn and start rushing back in.'

'So what do we do then? Drown?'

'Of course not, silly. We swim back to shore on an ingoing tide.'

'Sounds dodgy to me,' I said dubiously. 'How do you know all this nautical stuff anyway?'

'Dad's a keen yachtsman. I've been deep-sea cruising with him lots of times.'

'Well, hello sailor! You really think this will work?'

'Of course it will. We're both good swimmers. Besides, we don't really have to swim, just float. We go out on an outgoing tide, and in on an ingoing tide. What can go wrong? Trust me, it'll work.'

We loafed away the rest of the day at home and on the beach, waiting for nightfall and the low spring tide.

I had several more goes at reaching Skeff, and the last one produced disturbing news.

'I'm afraid he's in hospital,' said the worried receptionist's voice. 'He was attacked leaving the office last night. He's unconscious at the moment, suspected concussion, no visitors allowed.'

I told Cassie the news. 'Things are starting to turn ugly. We'll try this mad scheme of yours, but if that doesn't work that's it. We'll tell your mother what's been going on and head straight back to London, OK?'

'OK, Ben,' said Cassie. 'Don't worry, things will work out.'

She seemed to have some kind of inner confidence, as if her powers were telling her something. I could only hope she was right.

* * *

We passed a quiet and peaceful afternoon. It was almost like a holiday!

Insisting on doing her share, Cassie's mother rustled up a scratch supper of soup, baked beans on toast and tinned pineapple, from the tins in the store cupboard. Then she went back to work and eventually off to bed.

Cassie and I waited until late evening, then got into our swimming things and sneaked out of the house, heading for the beach.

We left a note for Cassie's mum on the kitchen table:

> *Gone for a moonlight swim. Don't worry, won't be late. Ben and Cassie.*

As Cassie had predicted, it was the lowest of low tides. What looked like miles and miles of sand stretched out to the distant sea.

When we finally reached the water's edge, only a narrow sea-filled gully separated us from the wreck. We swam across it with ease and climbed aboard the rusting remains of the *Nemesis*.

Salt-eroded iron struts creaked ominously under our weight.

I'd brought a torch in the waterproof pocket of my swimming trunks. I swung it around. There was little enough to see. The yacht was a broken-backed skeleton, with rusting steel ribs, and the remains of what must once have been cabins.

We searched it, centimetre by centimetre, and found nothing.

At last we stood in the remains of the main cabin, looking around us. By now the tide had turned and I could hear the sea rushing around the wreck, shaking the rusting skeleton. I felt a sudden stab of fear.

'We've got to go, Cassie,' I said urgently. 'If we're down here when the wreck floods, we could be trapped.'

'Another moment,' pleaded Cassie. 'It's close, I know it's close. I can feel it. Let me see if I can sense where it is . . .'

'All right, but hurry. If this wreck collapses, we'll still be here when the tide comes in and covers it again.'

Cassie stood in the middle of the wrecked main cabin, turning slowly round, concentrating, putting herself in a kind of trance.

Suddenly one of her arms rose as if of its own accord . . . She pointed upwards. 'Ben, that pipe . . .'

A rusting iron pipe ran across one corner of the cabin. What its purpose might have been I had no idea. Steam heating perhaps.

I jumped up and grabbed the pipe, heaving down on it as hard as I could. For a moment nothing happened. Then the pipe, weakened by fifty years of salt-sea erosion, creaked and broke away. Something dropped out of the open end – and Cassie caught it. I shone the torch on her find. It was a bottle, a little narrow bottle with a wax-sealed stopper.

'That's it,' whispered Cassie. 'I know that's it!'

Waves slammed against the ship, rocking the whole creaking structure. Even after all this time, it was still possible that the weakened skeleton would collapse on us.

I took the bottle from Cassie's hand.

'Maybe it is, but unless we get out of here we may never survive to find out.'

I thought for a moment, then unscrewed my torch. Hands trembling, I shook out the batteries and dropped the bottle in their place. It fitted neatly. I screwed the torch together and zipped it back into my waterproof pocket.

More waves crashed against the shattered wreck and there was an ominous creaking sound.

'Quick, let's get out of here,' I gasped.

We clambered back up on to the remains of the deck. From seaward, the whole ocean seemed to be rushing towards us. Waves crashed into the shattered hulk, making it groan and rock. Landwards, a stretch of shining moonlit water separated us from the land.

I turned and gave Cassie a quick hug. 'Congratulations, you did it! Now let's go home.'

Hand in hand, we jumped into the sea.

As Cassie had predicted, it was an easy swim on the ingoing tide.

Cassie was almost at the shoreline when she suddenly screamed and disappeared under the water. I swam towards her, and felt the undertow sucking me under as well.

Desperately fighting it, I struggled towards where Cassie had surfaced, gasping for air. I kicked out against another surge of the undertow – and felt sand under my feet.

'Cassie!' I shouted, and lunged towards her, grabbing her hand. 'Cassie! Don't try to swim. Stand up!'

The water was only chest high now. We both stood up and struggled slowly towards the shoreline, with the powerful undertow still trying to drag us back. We fought our way past it at last, and collapsed panting on the beach.

We had survived the perils of the sea. What we didn't know was that worse dangers were waiting for us on shore.

CHAPTER TEN

SHOWDOWN

We sneaked back into the house and crept up the stairs to get dry and dressed, scooping up the note I'd left for Cassie's mother on the way. If she hadn't seen it, she didn't need to see it, now we were safely back.

I dried quickly and dressed in jeans and a T-shirt. I picked up the torch, eager to examine its contents, then decided it was only fair to wait till we were all together.

I waited for Cassie and we went down into the kitchen. Cassie rushed to the stove and put the kettle on.

'Well done,' I said. 'What we both need is a hot drink.'

'Now,' said Cassie, gazing eagerly at the torch. 'Let's see what we've got.'

Cassie's mother came into the kitchen. She was still dressed, and had obviously been working late.

She looked at the torch in my hand. 'What's that for? Expecting a power cut?'

I was about to explain, when we heard the front door open and the sound of people coming into the house.

'Who the devil's that at this time of night?' said Mrs Sinclair indignantly. Before I could stop her, she shot out of the room to see what was going on.

I heard her angry voice from the hallway.

'Mr Daumier! What is the meaning of this intrusion? How did you get in?'

Then Richard Daumier's suave tones, 'You forget, Mrs Sinclair, this is still my house. Naturally I have a key.'

'It may be your house, but I am your guest, and I have a right to privacy.'

'So do I, but your daughter and her friend have chosen to breach it. Now you must all pay the penalty.'

I realised I was still holding the torch. Using the 'hide in plain sight' principle, I tossed it carelessly on the kitchen table.

I was just in time. Mrs Sinclair backed into the kitchen, followed by Richard Daumier, still wearing his country gentleman outfit. Behind him was Tubby Barker, the fat tattooed amusement arcade manager. He was carrying a shotgun and it was aimed at us.

Daumier surveyed us with a contemptuous sneer.

'Ah, the two juvenile troublemakers! Did you really think you could deceive *me*? I'm the Squire; I know everything that happens in Polzod. I know that old fool Pelligrew sold you the shipwreck book – he'll lose his shop for that. I have a friend at that rag the *Pioneer,* so I know about the e-mail your interfering friend Skeffington sent you. He too has been dealt with – not sufficiently, but that can be remedied.'

'Come on, he was just doing us a favour,' I protested. 'We were interested in the case and he passed on an old newspaper report. And all old Pelligrew did was sell us a book. It's all public information, where's the harm?'

'And did you enjoy your trip to the wreck? Oh yes, I've had you watched. What did you find there?'

'We didn't find anything because we weren't looking for anything,' said Cassie calmly. 'We just fancied a moonlight swim.'

'You were looking for evidence to use against me!' screamed Daumier. 'And you found nothing because there is nothing to find! I have searched that wreck many times over the years. If there ever was anything, it has all been destroyed by the sea long ago.'

He was talking to convince himself, I thought. He was still afraid – and totally paranoid. Hence the extreme reaction to any sign of interest in his past. If five years of guilt had driven Peter Daumier to suicide, fifty years of guilty knowledge had driven Richard Daumier quietly insane.

To my horror, he picked up the torch from the table and clicked the switch.

'It doesn't work.'

'I know,' I said carelessly. 'I dropped it. Bulb's gone, I think.'

He tossed the torch carelessly back on the table.

'I demand to know what's going on,' said Mrs Sinclair.

'If you don't know, dear lady, there's really no time to tell you. You will all come with me, please.'

'Where to?'

'A walk along the cliffs. A one-way walk, I'm afraid. Another tourist tragedy, caused by carelessness. When your bodies are found, I shall see there's an indignant editorial in the *Bugle,* demanding that Doombar Point be fenced off.'

For once even Mrs Sinclair was stunned into silence.

We filed out of the house, Daumier leading the way, Tubby Barker following behind with his shotgun.

As we walked along the moonlit cliff-path, summer lightning flashed, and thunder rumbled across the sky. Soon – all too soon – Doombar Point, also known as Maiden's Leap, came into sight.

'Listen,' I whispered, 'when we get to Maiden's Leap, scatter and run. He can't shoot three ways at once. I'll tackle Tubby.'

If I could make him fire both barrels in the air, someone might hear. In any case, he'd need time to reload, and that would give us a chance to escape.

Mrs Sinclair looked too stunned to take in what was happening.

Cassie, on the other hand, seemed strangely calm.

'Don't worry, Mum, Ben,' she said quietly. 'It'll be all right.'

'I wish I had your confidence,' I whispered.

'There's help on the way. I can feel it.'

'Silence!' snapped Daumier. He took up a position to one side of Maiden's Leap and beckoned us forward. 'Will you jump or will you be pushed? Go over you must, I'm afraid, dead or alive. You first, I think, young man.'

The shotgun jabbed me in the back and I took

several involuntary steps forward. I was close to the edge now. Another flash of lightning showed me waves pounding the jagged rocks below.

Suddenly Cassie shouted, 'Look, Mr Daumier, look!'

A white shape appeared in front of Daumier, a scrawny girl in a worn cotton nightgown. Her back was turned so we couldn't see her face – but Daumier could.

'Emily's come for you, Mr Daumier,' said Cassie in a high, clear voice. 'Emily, the girl you murdered fifty years ago, to save your family fortune. You always knew she'd come some day, didn't you? It's what you've been afraid of all these years.'

Richard Daumier backed away from the glowing white shape, trembling in fear.

'No!' he screamed. 'Keep her away from me!'

He backed away further, apparently unaware how close he was to the cliff-edge.

There was another crack of lightning and a split appeared in the ground before Daumier's feet. The split widened, and suddenly the piece of cliff that Daumier stood on crumbled away. A massive chunk of rock hurtled over the cliff to the rocks below, taking Daumier with it. We heard one last terrible scream as he disappeared.

The white shape faded away.

For a moment we stood there in astonished silence.

I turned and pushed aside the barrel of Tubby's shotgun.

'No point in killing us now,' I said reasonably. 'With Daumier dead, it's all over, there's nobody to pay you. I'd clear out if I were you.'

'Yeah, right,' he mumbled. 'No hard feelings.'

He hurried down the path towards Polzod.

I put my arms around Cassie and her mother and hugged them close, my legs feeling suddenly weak.

'It's over,' I said shakily. 'Let's go home.'

Back in the kitchen, over hot cups of tea, we examined the contents of the torch.

Mrs Sinclair shook the rolled-up letter from the bottle on to a sheet of newspaper. Carefully, she flattened it out.

The letter began, *I, Peter Daumier, unable to live with my guilt, hereby confess to the murder of my brother Simon, and to aiding and abetting my son Richard in the murder of Emily Tregorran, in order to conceal my crime by blaming her . . .*

The letter went on to describe exactly the sequence of events we'd seen through the eyes of the ghost. It told how Richard had used Emily's hand to plant her fingerprints on the candlestick and the quickly-forged confession, and then thrown her still-living body over the cliff at Doombar Point.

'Well, what do you think?' Cassie asked her mother. 'Is that substantial new evidence or what?'

'It will have to be authenticated,' said Mrs Sinclair. 'Handwriting, signature, paper, ink, even fingerprints, perhaps. But we can do all that. This is substantial new evidence all right. Now I can go to work.' She paused. 'The first thing to do is to contact the police . . .'

Go to work she did. With the full backing of the good old *News of the Screws* and her own considerable legal clout, she insisted on, and got, a full judicial enquiry.

The enquiry formally cleared Emily Tregorran's name, and accused Richard and his father Peter of both murders.

But that came later.

In Polzod meanwhile, Richard Daumier's criminal empire unravelled. His safe was crammed with incriminating papers. Out of sheer vanity he'd kept careful records of all his crimes.

Cousin Lavinia disappeared. Apparently she was heavily involved in all his criminal schemes. Some people said she'd really been the brains of the outfit.

Cousin Henry, who seemed completely innocent,

inherited the estate. He had no desire to break the trust. He planned to sell the Polzod mansion and move back into Doombar House.

So Cassie's mother lost a client, and the cliff area was safe from development.

Tubby Barker disappeared as well. One of his thugs, the one Cassie had punched, cracked under police questioning and confessed to getting Sam Turner, the London journalist, drunk and shoving him over the cliff.

Our journalist friend Skeff recovered from his concussion, and did brilliant coverage of the whole Daumier story. He ended up with a job in Fleet Street – working, of course, on the *News of the Screws*.

All this, too, came later.

Meanwhile Cassie and I finished our holiday. On our last day we took a final stroll along the cliff-top path, passing Maiden's Leap, now safely fenced off.

Suddenly Cassie pointed. 'Look!'

I looked.

Far down below, at the edge of the sea, a barefoot figure in white was paddling happily in the waves. She seemed to sense we were looking at her, and she turned and smiled and waved.

Then she faded gently away . . .

If you would like more information about
books available from Piccadilly Press and how
to order them, please contact us at:

Piccadilly Press Ltd.
5 Castle Road
London
NW1 8PR

Tel: 020 7267 4492
Fax: 020 7267 4493

Feel free to visit our website at
www.piccadillypress.co.uk

OCEAN S.O.S.

FOR MICHAEL AND PETER CULLUM, WITH GRATEFUL
THANKS FOR ALL YOUR EXPERT HELP.
LOVE FROM JAN AND SARA

AND FOR ALL THE CHARITIES THAT ARE WORKING
ON BEHALF OF DOLPHINS EVERYWHERE.

STRIPES PUBLISHING
An imprint of Magi Publications
1 The Coda Centre, 189 Munster Road,
London SW6 6AW

A paperback original
First published in Great Britain in 2010

Text copyright © Jan Burchett and Sara Vogler, 2010
Illustrations copyright © Diane Le Feyer of Cartoon Saloon, 2010
Cover illustration copyright © Andrew Hutchinson, 2010

ISBN: 978-1-84715-131-5

A CIP catalogue record for this book is available
from the British Library.

Printed and bound in the UK.

10 9 8 7 6 5 4 3 2

WILD
RESCUE
OCEAN S.O.S.

J. Burchett and S. Vogler

Stripes

STATUS: FILE CLOSED
LOCATION:
SICHUAN, CHINA
CODE NAME: JING JING

STATUS: FILE CLOSED
LOCATION:
SOUTH BORNEO
CODE NAME: KAWAN

STATUS: FILE CLOSED
LOCATION:
SUMATRA, INDONESIA
CODE NAME: TORA

STATUS: FILE CLOSED
LOCATION:
KENYA, AFRICA
CODE NAME: TOMBOI

RESCUE
MISSION DATABASE

CHAPTER ONE

"Ready, steady, dive!" yelled Zoe.

She plunged into the leisure centre pool just ahead of her twin brother, Ben. They sped through the water, until they reached the jacuzzi, their finishing line. Zoe slapped her hand on the wall.

"I won!" she declared.

"Only just," said Ben.

"What shall we do till the wave machine comes on?" asked Zoe, pushing her brown hair out of her eyes.

"More challenges," said Ben. "Bet I can

sit on the bottom and hold my breath longer than you."

"That's not fair," said Zoe. "You *always* win that one."

But Ben had already sucked in a huge mouthful of air and ducked down under the surface. Zoe joined him, and they sat on the floor of the pool. Zoe kept her back to her brother. She knew he'd do everything he could to make her laugh.

All of a sudden, someone tapped Ben on the shoulder. He whipped round to see a young woman in dark goggles peering straight at him. She gave him a thumbs up. Ben let out all his air in a stream of bubbles and burst to the surface.

Zoe was just behind him. "I won again!" she exclaimed.

"I had to come up," Ben panted. "Erika's here."

Zoe looked eagerly up and down the pool.

"I can't see her. You're just making up an excuse for losing."

"Over here!" came a voice with a slight German accent. Erika was peeping out from behind a fountain in the corner and waving a glass eyeball at them.

They swam across to her.

"Erika!" cried Ben. "So we've got a new mission!"

Zoe and Ben Woodward were like every other eleven-year-old, except for one important difference. They were operatives for Wild, a secret organization dedicated to saving animals all over the world. It had been set up by their godfather, Dr Stephen Fisher. Whenever they were needed he sent his second-in-command, Erika Bohn, to fetch them. But she was never allowed to tell them the details of their mission. Instead, he always sent them a glass eyeball – a clue to which animal they'd be trying to rescue.

"Good to see you both," said Erika. She peeled off her goggles and handed them the eyeball. It was a similar size to a human's and had an inky black pupil.

Zoe turned it over in her hand. "I wonder which animal this is from."

"You can think about that in the helicopter," said Erika. "Come on, let's get dressed and head off to Wild Island."

Twenty minutes later, they were flying out over the North Sea, their noses full of the familiar smell of chicken manure from the fuel – like everything at Wild, the helicopter was environmentally friendly.

Zoe took the chance to phone their grandmother while Ben examined the eyeball. The children's parents were vets who were currently working abroad and Gran had come to look after them while their parents were away. Mr and Mrs Woodward had no idea about their children's work for Wild and only Gran was in on their secret.

"That Stephen," came her cheerful voice through the speaker. "Where's he sending you now?"

"We don't know yet," said Zoe. "He's given us a clue, though."

"He was always one for a puzzle!" Gran laughed. "Look after yourselves. I'll see you when you get back."

Ben held up the eyeball. Suddenly, the pupil caught the light and glowed.

"It's got eyeshine," said Ben. "You know, like a cat or a dog when you catch them in a torch beam. It helps them to see in the dark."

Zoe took a look. "What other animals have that?" she asked.

"I'm thinking," said Ben. "Quite a few mammals – and fish."

"Don't forget to see what your uncle has to say," said Erika, pointing towards a hollow in the console.

Ben put the eyeball into it. At once, a hologram of their godfather appeared.

"Hello, godchildren," he said. "Have you worked out what it is yet? You might need a clue. It's—"

The image began to flicker. Uncle Stephen's faint voice could just be heard. "Something wrong with the hologram recorder. Wish I hadn't spilt my tea on it…"

The hologram disappeared.

Zoe laughed. "Uncle Stephen may be brilliant, but he's very clumsy. We'll just have to wait."

"Wild Island coming up," called Erika.

She brought the helicopter down to land. As soon as they'd disembarked, she pressed a button on a hand-held remote, activating the mechanism that brought up the fake shed to hide the helicopter. They made their way across to what looked like an outdoor toilet, but in fact hid a supersonic lift.

The children felt their stomachs lurch as they zoomed down into the headquarters of Wild. The lift doors opened, and they found themselves face to face with their godfather. He was wearing a lab coat over bright shorts and a bobble hat rammed down over his spiky red hair.

"Greetings, godchildren!" he cried. "Now come with me. There's no time to lose."

They hurried along the corridor and took turns placing their fingertips on a small pad next to a door marked "Control Room". As soon as their prints had been identified, the door slid open to reveal the large bright room that was the technological centre of Wild. Consoles and lights flashed. Operatives were working at keyboards, but they all paused to give Ben and Zoe a cheery wave. Uncle Stephen led the children over to his desk.

"Sorry about the hologram," he said. "What did you make of the eye?"

Ben told them what they had deduced
so far.

"Good, good," murmured their godfather.
"Well then?"

"It's very hard," said Erika. "Come on,
give them their clue."

Uncle Stephen stroked his chin. "Although
this animal is a mammal, it lives in the sea."

"There are quite a few sea mammals," said
Ben.

"But this one's particularly intelligent,"
their godfather told them.

"Got it," cried Zoe immediately. "We're
rescuing a dolphin!"

CHAPTER TWO

"Well done," said Uncle Stephen. "I knew my clever godchildren would get the answer!"

Zoe tugged at his sleeve. "Tell us the details!" she said impatiently.

"I want you to look at this," said Uncle Stephen, pointing to a huge wall monitor displaying a website for a marine park. The park looked bright and welcoming, with the slogan – "Mundo Marino, the jewel of the Caribbean Coast".

"We have an operative who keeps track of

what goes on in water parks and zoos all over the world," Uncle Stephen explained. "She picked up reports of problems at this place in Mexico."

"Is that where the dolphin is?" said Zoe. "I hate seeing them in captivity, but we can't rush in and kidnap one."

"That's not the problem," said her godfather. "The park doesn't look like that now. It's been closed down."

"It used to be run by an old man who loved all forms of marine life," explained Erika. "I don't approve of dolphins being kept in captivity either, but Señor Delgado was doing a good job."

Uncle Stephen took up the story. "He died six months ago and his son took it over. He didn't spend enough money on the park and if any member of staff complained, he sacked them. By the time the authorities found out and closed it down many animals were in a terrible state."

"That's disgusting!" exclaimed Ben.

"And the tale gets worse," Uncle Stephen continued. "Of the four bottlenose dolphins there, only one – a four-year-old male called Fingal – was left alive. He's said to have a scar running from his right eye to just below his mouth, so he must have been mistreated."

"How awful!" cried Zoe. "So it's poor Fingal we've got to rescue. But if the park's been closed, where is he now?"

"We don't know," answered Erika. "When the owner knew the authorities were on to him he dumped all the animals in the ocean, even though Fingal was born in captivity. He's in prison now, thank goodness."

Uncle Stephen tapped a key and a map of the Caribbean Sea appeared on the screen. He indicated a point on the south-east coast of Mexico. "San Miguel – where Fingal was dumped four days ago."

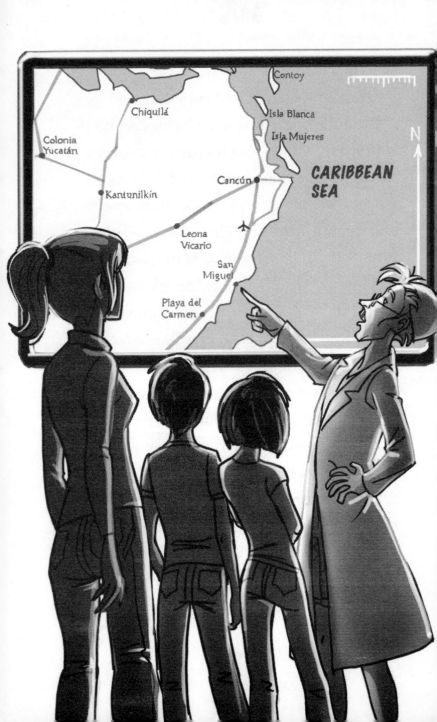

"So he could be anywhere in the Caribbean by now," said Ben.

"We don't think he's gone far, and that's part of the problem," said Uncle Stephen. "We've been monitoring local radio reports and it seems that a young dolphin has been bothering fishermen in San Miguel. We think this must be Fingal. He seems to be after their catch."

"Fingal was born in the park so he would naturally go to humans for his food, rather than hunting for himself," added Erika.

"The fishermen won't like that," said Zoe.

"You're right," said Uncle Stephen. "And that's why your mission is so urgent. Fingal will either get hurt or caught in a net if he's not rescued soon. And there's always the danger of a shark attacking a young dolphin living without the protection of a pod. Fingal needs rehabilitation before he's fit to live in the wild."

"Who does that sort of rehabilitation?" asked Ben.

"There's the Agua Clara Dolphin Sanctuary about fifty kilometres from there – near Cancun," said Uncle Stephen, "but they haven't got the time or resources to travel all that way to search for a dolphin in trouble. However, I can think of one way they would find him very quickly. If he was tracked down and enticed to stay somewhere by two very clever young Wild operatives until the centre could come and get him…"

"Well, Ben." Zoe winked at her twin brother. "I wonder who our godfather has in mind to do the tracking?"

"I suppose we could do it, Zoe," replied Ben, with a cheeky grin. "We're not very busy and it *is* the summer holidays…"

Uncle Stephen beamed at them. "I knew my wonderful godchildren would be up for it."

"When do we head off?" asked Zoe eagerly.

"We'll be leaving for San Miguel as soon as you've got all your kit," said Erika. "Fingal needs our help as soon as possible. I'll pretend to be your aunt who's kind enough to take you for a holiday while I work. I'm going to pose as an environmentalist."

"You *are* an environmentalist!" Uncle Stephen laughed. "And your reason for being in a Mexican fishing village is genuine." He turned to Ben and Zoe. "I've been looking into the problem of dolphins being caught in fishing nets for some time. There are nets that emit the call of a much larger marine mammal so that dolphins are warned to stay well away. But these can be too expensive for poor fishing communities like those around the San Miguel area. I've developed my own version that is foolproof and much cheaper."

"I'm going to offer the fishermen a free trial," said Erika. "And while I'm doing that, you can search for Fingal."

"It'll be awesome out on the sea," said
Ben. "Will we get to do some snorkelling?"

Uncle Stephen rubbed his hands together.
"You certainly will – and you can use my
latest invention."

He opened a drawer and rummaged about
in the mess. Finally, he pulled out two
snorkels and some flippers. He handed them
to Ben and Zoe.

"I've got news for you, Uncle Stephen,"
said Zoe. "Snorkels have already been
invented."

"These may look like any other snorkel,"
said their godfather. "But they're not. They're
GILS – Great Integrated Life Support.
Unlike a snorkel, this will give you ten
minutes of oxygen." Uncle Stephen pointed
to Zoe's device. "See the little capsule here in
the mouthpiece? This is a special compressed
air tank. All you have to do is go back up to

the surface and it refills automatically. I've set
it to give you a strong taste of peppermint
when the air is about to run out. And if you
look at the mask, you'll see it's designed to
give enhanced underwater visibility."

"And let's guess, these are no ordinary
flippers either," said Ben.

"Indeed." Uncle Stephen beamed. "They're
extra streamlined for increased speed."

"Cool!" said Ben, slipping on the flippers
and waddling round the room. "They feel
really light – and strong."

"What sort of boat will we be going out in?" asked Zoe.

"A speedboat?" said Ben hopefully.

"Don't be daft." Zoe laughed. "The engine would frighten Fingal off."

"Zoe's right," said Erika. "I'll be organizing a sailing dinghy for you."

"Perfect!" Zoe punched the air.

Ben grinned. "You would say that."

"I bet you wish you'd done those sailing courses with me last summer," said Zoe.

Erika delved into Uncle Stephen's drawer and, after removing two apple cores and an old milk carton, produced what looked like two hand-held game consoles. She held them out to the children. "Of course you can't go without your BUGs."

Ben and Zoe's BUGs – Brilliant Undercover Gizmos – were technological wonders. They had inbuilt communicators, satellite tracking, translators and countless

other useful functions. They even had one
or two games.

"Wait a minute," said Ben. "Are these
still going to work in the sea?"

"They are waterproof," said Uncle
Stephen. "I've tested them in the bath."
His eyes twinkled. "In fact, you'd better call
them Brilliant Underwater Gizmos for this
mission!"

Ben and Zoe groaned.

"I've added a limpet," he went on. "It's a
wireless extension of your BUGs."

Zoe turned her gizmo over in her hand.
"Is it this?" she said, peeling off a circular
coin-sized piece of rubber with a metal
device embedded in it.

"That's right," said Uncle Stephen. "It's
designed to stick to the side of your boat by
giving off a slimy substance just like a
limpet does. It transmits and identifies calls
underwater. All the info will be displayed

on your BUG screens, in the usual way."

"Great," said Zoe.

"You'll also have a supply of treats to lure Fingal to you," Erika told them.

"I knocked up the recipe myself," Uncle Stephen added. "They're only tasty to dolphins."

"Good," said Zoe. "So we won't be chased by shoals of tuna!"

"Time for you to be off then," said Uncle Stephen. "The Wild Jet is fuelled and ready to go, and Fingal's depending on you."

"I think there's something you've forgotten to tell them, Dr Fisher," said Erika.

"Surely not," Uncle Stephen replied, looking puzzled.

"The weather?"

"Oh yes!" exclaimed their godfather. "Well done, Erika. It's hurricane season in the Caribbean."

"Thanks for the warning!" exclaimed Ben.

Uncle Stephen frowned. "I hope that hasn't put you off."

"No way!" cried Zoe. "Fingal, here we come!"

CHAPTER THREE

Zoe pulled on her T-shirt and shorts over her wetsuit, and looked out of the guest house window at the clear blue sky.

"It's a lovely day," she said. "Light breeze. Good sailing weather. Perfect for our mission."

The children and Erika had arrived at the Casa Blanca guest house in San Miguel late last night. It had been dark when they'd taken the taxi from the airfield where Erika had left the Wild plane. The proprietor, Señor Rodriguez, had greeted them in excellent English and made them welcome with hot drinks and a big plate of biscuits. Breakfast that morning had been just as delicious.

"Come on, Zoe," said Ben impatiently. "Let's go."

"Don't be so hasty." Zoe laughed. "We must do a final check of our equipment first."

She sat on her bed and lifted her backpack up beside her.

"First-aid kit, binoculars, GILs…" she said.

"…flippers, diving belt with knife, treats for Fingal," muttered Ben, as he carefully repacked each one. "How's your Spanish?"

"I can say please and thank you," said Zoe.

"How about – do you know where the missing dolphin is because we've come to rescue him and get him to a rehabilitation centre?" Ben said teasingly.

"I'll leave that to you!" Zoe came back quickly.

Ben picked up his BUG and peeled off a small plastic earpiece from the side. "At least with our translators we can make sure that we understand everything we hear," he said, putting it in his ear.

Zoe did the same and they turned on their BUGs' translation mode.

Just then, Ben's BUG vibrated.

"Message from Erika," he reported. "Sailing dinghy hired. It's down on the jetty."

"I wonder how she's getting on at her meeting with the fishermen," said Zoe, tucking her flippers, mask and snorkel into her bag. "It's lucky *her* Spanish is good. I wouldn't like to try explaining how Uncle Stephen's nets work!"

Erika had wasted no time. After breakfast, she'd set off for a large fishing village along the coast to start her campaign of persuading the fishermen to use the new nets.

Ben hoisted his backpack on to his shoulders. "Let's see what we can find out about Fingal from the local people."

"Good idea," said Zoe, as they made their way down to reception.

"And while we're in the village we could buy some food," added Ben.

"You've only just had breakfast!" exclaimed Zoe. "You can't still be hungry. That hot chocolate and those spicy tortillas were very filling."

"I'm just thinking about lunch," said Ben.

Señor Rodriguez came out to take their key.

He looked at the children's bulging backpacks. "Are you off on a long trip?"

"We're going sailing," said Zoe. "Our aunt's hiring us a boat. The sea looks very clear here – not like back in England – and we want to see the underwater life."

"My sister has always dreamed of seeing

wild dolphins," Ben explained. "She'd better be lucky or I'll never hear the end of it!"

"You could be lucky," said Señor Rodriguez. "The fishermen often see them from their boats. But listen, your aunt might not have to take you that far out. You might even see the dolphin from the old marine park."

"How come?" asked Zoe.

Señor Rodriguez told them all about the closing of the marine park. Ben and Zoe pretended it was news to them. "The dolphin's been popping up ever since. Only yesterday, Filiberto was telling me how it was pestering him when he was out with his rod and line. It was a nuisance, he said. It kept calling to him and banging against the side of the boat. Then it did a funny sort of backwards walk on its tail."

"That does sound like a tame dolphin," said Zoe.

"You be careful now," he added. "Dolphins are one thing, but there are also sharks further out beyond the bay. So no swimming off the boat."

"We'll look out for sharks," said Ben.

The children set off for the sea.

They walked along a rough, dusty road towards the centre of San Miguel, where houses were scattered around an old church. The morning sun shone warmly on their red tiled roofs.

Ben and Zoe rounded a corner and gasped in delight. Ahead of them lay the turquoise waters of the Caribbean, sparkling in the sunshine. A few guest houses and tourist shops overlooked the ocean, but there were no holidaymakers around. The bay was wide, with a wooden jetty and boats bobbing in the gentle swell, tethered to red buoys. Several fishing vessels were heading towards shore, bringing in their catches. The children could hear the distant drone of their engines. Far out to sea they could just make out a small island, scattered with palm trees.

"That's a coral island," Ben told his sister. "I read about it on the plane."

Zoe trained her binoculars on the headland at the far end of the bay where a

battered fence surrounded some shabby
buildings. A tatty sign hung lopsidedly
on its hinges.

"That's Mundo Marino," she said in
disgust. "So that's where poor Fingal was
living."

"We'll soon have him in a much better place than that!" said Ben.

They made their way down the main street, past gift shops, a bar and several food stores.

Some of the shopkeepers were fixing wooden shutters over the windows. "Everywhere's closing," exclaimed Zoe in surprise.

A small supermarket was shuttered up like the others, but still had the door open.

"At least we can buy our food here," said Ben, as he pushed open the door and breathed in the delicious smell of freshly baked bread and smoked meats.

"Hello," Zoe said to the woman behind the counter, as Ben looked longingly at the filled pastries laid out in front of them. "Do you speak English?"

The woman nodded. "A little," she answered.

"Why is everything closing?" Zoe went on, pointing to the shutters.

"Hurricane," said the woman, with an apologetic smile.

Zoe turned to Ben. "This is really bad news," she whispered in alarm. "Fingal isn't used to being in the sea, let alone in hurricane conditions!"

CHAPTER FOUR

"We've got to get Fingal to the centre before the hurricane arrives," muttered Ben. "If he stays near the shoreline he'll find it hard to swim in the strong waves – and there's always bits of wood and rubbish that get stirred up in storms. He could get hurt."

"Let's hope there's time," answered Zoe. "First we need to know when it's going to hit. Hurry up and pick what you want. Then we'll ask."

She quickly found fruit, crisps and bottles of water, while Ben pointed to the biggest pastries on display. They were stuffed with chicken and cream cheese.

"Pastelitos," said the shop owner, as she wrapped them up. "Very good."

"When is the hurricane coming?" asked Zoe, as she paid.

"Hurricane … it … is…" The woman gave up her attempt at English. She led them to the door and nodded towards a nearby café. There was a terrace outside but all the tables and chairs had been cleared away.

"Good English!" she said, pointing at the café owner, who was putting up a last shutter. "He say."

They thanked her and made for the café. The trees were swaying a little in the breeze, but the sky was blue.

"There's no sign of a storm," said Ben.

The café owner smiled as they approached. He was a friendly-looking man with brown eyes that sparkled above an impressive moustache.

"Can you help us?" said Zoe. "We've heard there's a hurricane coming. Surely it can't be. The weather looks so calm."

"We have a report from the National Hurricane Centre. We might be at the edge of one," he told them. "So we take precautions. The report said it passes close by this afternoon, but we make sure we are ready in good time."

"That's a relief," said Zoe. "We should be able to get some sailing in this morning then."

"You don't seem too worried about the storm," said Ben to the café owner.

The man gave a shrug. "We are used to it. The storm comes, we pack away. The storm goes, we open up again. What else can we do?"

At that moment, a man in fisherman's overalls stuck his head round the door and called out to him in Spanish. Ben and Zoe's BUGs translated the words. "News just in, Enrico. The hurricane's heading north. It's giving us a miss this time."

Enrico told Ben and Zoe the news. "You will be able to enjoy your sailing," he said. He began to take down the shutters from the window. "And if you see some strange dead fish, do not worry. There is nothing wrong with the water – they were, how do you say, thrown out from Mundo Marino."

"We've heard about that," said Ben.

"But be careful of the tame dolphin," Enrico warned them. "It could upset a small boat. The fishermen are cross with it."

"They won't hurt it, will they?" said Zoe.

The café owner shrugged. "They have a living to earn and that is hard enough here."

He picked up a table and carried it outside.

"Poor Fingal," said Zoe. "All he's trying to do is get food."

"And that's all the fishermen are trying to do," Ben answered.

"*Graçias*," Zoe called to the café owner. "Thanks for your help."

The children raced along the rough bay road towards the wooden jetty stretching out from the beach.

"I really wish I'd done those sailing courses with you," panted Ben, as they ran. "Football seemed like more fun at the time."

"Don't worry," Zoe told him. "Just do as I say and it'll be fine. You can be my cabin boy."

"Great!" groaned Ben. "That's just an excuse to boss me about!"

There was a worn sign in English and Spanish saying "boats for hire", with an arrow pointing along the jetty.

A small single-masted sailing boat was moored at the end. Its green paintwork was peeling and two narrow benches ran along the inside. A dark-haired woman in shorts and a bright top gave Ben and Zoe a wave, as they walked down the jetty.

"That must be our boat," said Ben. "*La Gaviota.*"

"Looks a bit basic, but she's just the right size for the two of us," said Zoe.

"Boat for Bohn?" the woman said in halting English. "One day's hire?"

"That's right," said Zoe eagerly. "We'll be taking a trip up the coast."

"Your aunt said you can sail." The woman looked at them doubtfully and muttered in her own language. "So young."

Ben gulped.

"I have done exams," Zoe told her truthfully.

"That is good." The woman handed over two life jackets. "You wear these always. That is the rule."

Ben and Zoe slipped on the orange jackets.

"Thank you," said Zoe. She bent down,

pulled in the mooring rope and held the pointed prow of the boat firmly. She dropped their two backpacks into the bottom of the boat and nodded to her brother. "Go on, Ben. Climb aboard."

The boat owner folded her arms and
watched grimly. It was clear that she was
going to make sure her craft was safe in
the hands of two children. Trying to
look as if he knew what he was doing,
Ben clambered on to the dinghy,
which rocked violently.

"Whoa!" Arms flailing, he
made a grab for the mast and
clung to it in desperation.

"My brother likes to joke!" Zoe said quickly, as Ben threw himself on to one of the benches and gave a sheepish grin. She noticed that the woman didn't smile.

But before she could say anything, Zoe swiftly untied the rope and boarded the boat. First she rigged the sails, then she climbed to the stern and took hold of the tiller. As the sails caught the wind, she headed the boat out into the middle of the bay.

"Got away with it so far!" said Ben, looking back. "But she's still staring. What can I do to show her how expert I am?"

"Take that sheet and control the jib," Zoe told him, nodding towards the small triangular sail at the prow.

"Sheet?" Ben reached forward and grabbed the bottom of the front sail. "I'm not sure I can hold on for long," he said, as he wrestled with the flapping canvas. "It's pulling away."

Zoe burst out laughing. "The sheet is the rope that controls a sail. It's down there, secured to the side. Release it from its cleat – that's clip to landlubbers like you."

"Just testing!" Ben freed the rope and grinned at her. "And I'd like to see you explain the offside rule! Anyway, time for business. We've got to scour this bay for Fingal."

"We'll start around those fishing boats moored over there," said Zoe. "Get ready to go about. That means letting go of your rope when I tell you and moving to the other side of the dinghy. Oh, and mind the big wooden thing that swings across."

"The boom, you mean?" said Ben. "I do know that one!" His feet kicked something under the seat and he pulled it out. It was a pail, attached to a long piece of rope which was tied to a hook. "A bucket?" he asked. "Is that in case we're seasick?"

"It's for bailing out water, silly," said Zoe.
"Fix our backpacks to that hook, too.
Everything has to be battened down." She
looked ahead. "OK, ready about? Lee ho."

"Show off," said Ben.

"All right then." Zoe grinned. "Look out,
we're turning."

Zoe pushed the tiller away from her. The
boom moved over the boat, and the
children clambered across and took up the
sheets on the other side.

Taken by the gentle wind, the dinghy
moved among the rocking fishing boats
that were moored to buoys in the water.
Ben slipped his BUG out of his
backpack, scrolled through the animal
identification menu and set it to pick up
dolphin calls. Then he peeled the limpet
from his BUG, reached over the side of
the boat and stuck it to the hull beneath
the waterline.

"Nothing yet," Ben said, peering at the BUG screen.

"Let's get further out and try again," said Zoe, adjusting the mainsail to catch the light breeze.

As they reached the last buoy before open sea, a message appeared on his screen.

"The limpet's picked something up," he exclaimed. "It's a dolphin and it's close!"

CHAPTER FIVE

They peered eagerly out across the water.
Just a few metres away, the surface erupted
and a sleek grey dolphin leaped up in an
elegant arc and plunged back into the
waves. They could see it streaking through
the clear water close to the boat.

"Could that be Fingal?" gasped Zoe in
excitement.

"It looks like an adult," said Ben
doubtfully.

As he spoke, more fully-grown dolphins
burst to the surface.

"It's a pod," gasped Zoe. "Of course, now we've come further out we're going to pick up all the dolphins in the area."

The streamlined shapes shot along next to the dinghy, launching themselves out of the water and diving back with barely a splash.

"It looks as if they're racing us!" exclaimed Ben.

"Well, we don't stand a chance," replied Zoe, with a grin.

The dolphins criss-crossed in the air in front of the boat and then, as suddenly as they had come, they were gone.

Zoe stared after them. "What a display. They didn't need whistles and rewards like captive dolphins. They were *sooo* beautiful."

Ben grinned and rolled his eyes. "Off to Gooey City!" he groaned. "Although I have to agree they were amazing."

"Wouldn't it be great if Fingal could be part of a group like that one day," sighed Zoe.

"We'd better wait a bit before we try and listen for him," said Ben. "We'll just pick up that lot again."

"I'll head towards the bay," said Zoe. "He must be there somewhere."

They sailed up and down between the

buoys, but no light appeared on the BUG screen.

"I think we're in the wrong place," said Ben at last. "We've been searching for over an hour and there's no sign of Fingal."

Suddenly, they heard a distant shout from across the water. They looked up to see a small boat out beyond the bay. They could hear the chug of its engine.

"Fishing boat," remarked Zoe. "It must be coming back with its catch."

Then there was silence as someone turned the power off.

"Looks like they've got a problem with their net," said Ben.

Two of the crew were desperately trying to pull up a bright green fishing net, while a third was calling instructions and trying to keep the lurching vessel balanced.

Ben and Zoe could make out a few words, translated by the BUG.

"Something's caught."

"It's big."

"It's struggling. It'll pull us over."

Ben got out his binoculars. "Can't see what they've picked up," he reported anxiously, "but it's certainly in trouble." He glanced down at his BUG screen. "I should have checked sooner. It's saying 'dolphin'!"

"It could be Fingal," cried Zoe. "Watch out for the boom!" The boat swung round and Zoe edged it towards the struggling fishermen.

"The BUG's identified it as a distress cry," Ben told her. "Even if it's not Fingal, we've got to get in there and do something."

He pressed some buttons. "I'm saving that call just in case. All dolphins have a different signature call and if this is Fingal, we'll be able to identify him later."

Zoe steered the dinghy toward the buoys in the bay. Lowering the sails, she secured the boat to the nearest one, while Ben got out their GILS and flippers.

"If only I had my sailing knife with me," said Zoe. "We could use it to cut the net."

"I've got something even better," said Ben. "My diver's knife." He produced a sheathed knife from the backpack and strapped it to his belt.

"Remember what Señor Rodriguez told us," said Zoe. "Keep an eye out for sharks."

Ben nodded and ripped off his life jacket and clothes. "Sorry, Mrs Boat Owner," he muttered, as he pulled the mask on and adjusted the snorkel, "but there are times when you have to break the rules."

He fixed his BUG to his diving belt with a safety cord. Zoe did the same.

"Don't forget you've only got ten minutes' air," Zoe warned him.

Ben made a circle with his thumb and forefinger – the diver's sign for OK – and plunged into the water.

The water rushed into his ears as he sank into the clear sea. Bubbles streamed up in front of his face, and when they cleared he spotted the long, dark shape of the fishing boat in the water ahead. With the GILS, he found he was able to breathe as if he had an oxygen tank.

The water was very clear, so Ben made sure that he kept on the side of the boat away from the fishermen so they wouldn't spot him. But now he had a good view of the net. It was swollen with fish, and thrashing violently. As he came closer he could just see the terrified eye of a dolphin in the middle of the catch.

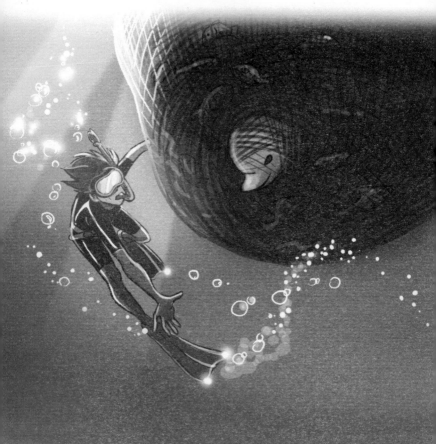

As he saw Zoe approaching, Ben jerked a thumb up, and they swam for the surface, making sure to stay out of sight of the fishermen.

"The dolphin's badly tangled in the fishing net," he told his sister, as they trod water side by side. "The more it tries to free itself the worse it gets. There's no way it can escape on its own."

"Poor thing," gasped Zoe. "Is it Fingal?"

"Can't tell," answered Ben. "We'll have to go back down. I'll use my knife to cut it free, but we mustn't be seen."

"Agreed," nodded Zoe. "We'll approach from underneath the hull – but keep away from the propeller."

They dived under the bottom of the fishing boat.

Zoe checked for holes in the nylon mesh, and signalled a negative to Ben.

Ben held the net to steady himself as he

pulled his knife from its sheath. The net gave a great lurch and the dolphin's head appeared, as it pushed its nose desperately against its prison.

Ben tugged at Zoe's arm and pointed to a jagged scar running from its eye to just below its mouth.

They had found Fingal!

CHAPTER SIX

This isn't working, thought Ben, as he worked away with the knife. *The more frightened Fingal becomes, the more he tangles himself up. If we don't free him soon, he'll run out of air.*

Cutting a net underwater was slippery work without a terrified dolphin to contend with. Each time Ben tried to break the net, Fingal would thrash, and he narrowly escaped cutting his hand. He'd lost his grip on his knife several times and it would have been on the seabed by now if it hadn't been attached to his belt by a cord.

Fingal writhed again and Ben nicked his hand with the knife. Ignoring the stinging pain, he attacked the net again and managed to slice through two strands.

Zoe could see how Fingal's struggles were hampering the rescue attempt. She swam to where his head was caught. He stared at her for a moment with frantic eyes, then started wriggling again. Zoe caught his snout through the net and patted his head.

Fingal calmed down a little. Ben cut through another strand, then another and tugged at the broken threads.

Zoe helped Ben tear at the thick nylon net. And suddenly Fingal thrust his snout through. The children ripped the hole wider, feeling the harsh nylon digging into their hands. At last they managed to drag it over the dolphin's head. After another tug, his flippers were free. But now the net was caught on his dorsal fin. Ben and Zoe took hold of the net and pulled hard. With a flick of his tail, Fingal burst through the hole and shot up to the surface.

But now Zoe was worried. When the fishermen saw the young dolphin and the hole in their net they might be angry enough to do something nasty to him. The net was rising slowly through the water, fish spilling out as the men winched it up. Zoe swam up on the other side of the boat to look for Fingal and lure him away. There he was, leaping in and out of the water, trying to attract the attention of the fishermen. Luckily, they were too busy cursing at the loss of their catch to notice him.

Zoe waved frantically at Fingal and then dived under the water. To her huge relief, the dolphin came swimming towards her. *His face looks as though he's grinning,* thought Zoe. He nudged her gently in the tummy and then swam on his back. She dived down deeper, and he followed. *He's used to humans,* she thought. *We'll have no trouble keeping him with us.*

She could see Ben now. But he seemed to be still fiddling with the net. And then she saw why. The cord securing his knife to his belt had tangled in it. He was stuck.

Ben was struggling desperately to free his knife. He could unclip the cord and swim away, leaving the knife in the nylon mesh, but the fishermen would be sure to see it and know that the net had been tampered with. What's more, Ben couldn't risk losing the knife. He didn't know when he might need it again.

Then he tasted peppermint. The GIL was running out of air. He tore at the net. He was having to hold his breath now. He was good at that, but would it be enough?

He felt a hand on his. It was Zoe. She worked with nimble fingers, nudging Fingal away when he got too close. At last, the knife was free. And just in time – the net shot up above the surface, sending Ben somersaulting backwards through the water.

Ben and Zoe were just about to kick away from the boat when a tremendous roar filled their ears and the water churned around them. The propeller was beginning to turn. Now that what was left of the catch was in, the fishermen had started their engine.

Whoosh! Fingal was gone, terrified by the noise and sudden swirling of the water. Above them, the boat began to move.

Ben kicked away hard to avoid the blades. His lungs were bursting now. He thrashed to the surface and gulped the air in relief.

Zoe swam up alongside him. "Are you all right?" she asked.

"I'm fine," said Ben, "now that I've got some air."

"Where's the blood coming from?"

Ben looked at the cut on his hand. "It's nothing," he assured her. "I nicked myself with my knife. The important thing is, where's Fingal now?"

"We'll be able to search for him better when we're back in the dinghy," said Zoe. "He can't be far away."

As they swam, Ben looked around. "You're right! I think I can see his fin," he said, pointing at the horizon. "And he's heading towards us at speed."

Zoe trod water and checked her BUG. "That's not Fingal," she said. "In fact it's not a dolphin at all. Swim for the boat!"

"What's the matter?" said Ben.

"It's a shark!"

CHAPTER SEVEN

Ben and Zoe thrashed through the waves, the water pounding in their ears. Even with their superfast flippers they were no match for the expert underwater killer that was streaking towards them, attracted by the blood. Ben couldn't stop himself taking a quick glance backwards under the surface. He wished he hadn't. He caught sight of the shark's tiny eyes and needle-sharp teeth. Surely it would reach them before they could get to safety. He kicked desperately – he wasn't going to be shark food!

Zoe reached the dinghy first. Ben saw her legs disappearing from the water as she scrambled aboard. With a final burst of energy, he launched himself at the boat. He felt a surge behind him as the shark lunged for him.

He tried to pull himself up out of the water, but in his panic he lost his grip on the side of the boat and plunged back in. He could see the ominous grey shape of the shark circling beneath him, ready to attack again. The blood from his hand was trailing out in a thin ribbon, exciting the hungry predator. Ben clawed at the side of the dinghy, kicking in desperation. Then, just as the shark lunged, he felt Zoe clutch his arm and pull him to safety.

Ben tumbled on to the deck, as the shark cannoned into the boat. He lay there, panting, while Zoe clung fearfully to the side and watched the grey body whipping round this way and that, battering the craft as it tried to locate its prey.

"We've got to get away!" she gasped. "It could capsize the dinghy."

Shaking, she clambered on to her seat, pulled off her snorkelling gear and put up the sails. Soon the dinghy was nipping over the waves away from the bay. But the shark wasn't giving up. Its grey fin could be seen copying every course change they made.

Ben scrolled down the menu of his BUG. "It's a bull shark," he read from the screen. "They often attack without provocation. So my blood must have really stirred it up."

"It's coming straight for us," yelled Zoe.

"It's going to ram us again!" cried Ben.

The shark slowed just before it reached them and swerved away.

"That was a practice run, I think," said Zoe. "Look, it's coming again."

"I'll find a predator to scare it," muttered Ben, scrolling through the BUG menu, his fingers slipping in his haste.

Now the shark was almost upon them, its fin cutting through the water like a blade.

"I've set the limpet to give out a killer whale sound," he said quickly. "I hope it works. The bull shark isn't frightened of many creatures."

The sound must have reached the shark because it suddenly changed course. With a flick of its powerful tail, it was gone.

"Good thinking," said Zoe in relief.

"Thanks for earlier," Ben said. "You saved my life."

Zoe shrugged. "Who's going to scrub the decks if my cabin boy gets eaten by a shark?"

Ben laughed. "I'll do it the minute we've found Fingal."

"That's not going to be so easy," said Zoe seriously. "He was badly scared by that boat engine. He could be a long way off by now."

"Remember what the lady at the hire place told us." Ben removed his mask and flippers, then threw Zoe her life jacket. They put them back on, tying the straps firmly.

At that moment, they heard an engine.

"Look out," said Ben. "There's a cabin cruiser approaching."

"Ahoy there!" came a cry.

A man stood at the cruiser's prow. The vessel came alongside and they heard the engine slowing.

"Don't forget, we're just dumb tourists," Zoe muttered to Ben.

"Not hard for you," Ben muttered back.

The man peered down at *La Gaviota* over the side of the cruiser.

"Do you speak English?" he called loudly and slowly. He had an American accent. He was joined by a woman in dark sunglasses.

Zoe grinned. "We *are* English."

"We thought we'd better check on you," said the man. "We were surprised to see you out here. You're very young to be out on your own."

"Don't worry about us," called Ben good-naturedly. "My sister's an expert sailor. She's got all sorts of badges."

"We're just having a little sail before heading back to San Miguel," said Zoe. "I'm teaching my brother the basics, so we're staying out of the bay to avoid the other boats. He's taking a long time to learn."

The woman laughed as Ben pretended to get himself tangled up in the ropes.

"Well, don't go out any further," said the man. "Stefano, our captain, told us that there's a hurricane on its way. It's not going to hit the coast, but it'll pass quite close and you'll feel the effects if you head into deeper water. You'd better follow us back to San Miguel. We're heading in now, just to be on the safe side."

The children were silent for a moment,
trying to think of what to say.

"That's really kind of you," said Zoe at
last. "But … we're…"

"She means our aunt's not far away in her
boat," Ben put in quickly. "We'll wait and
sail in with her. Thanks anyway."

"Your aunt?" said the woman doubtfully.
"We didn't see any other small dinghies."

"Are you sure?" said Ben. He slapped his
forehead. "Of course! We've been heading
for San Miguel and she said San Pedro.
We'd better turn round and get going."

Zoe didn't need telling twice. Soon the
dinghy was scooting over the waves. They
were relieved to see the cruiser continue
on its course for the bay.

"We didn't need that delay," said Zoe.
"But well done for getting us out of a
difficult spot. Now they've gone we can
search for Fingal again."

"But first I'm going to check where the hurricane is," said Ben. He called up the satellite weather map on his BUG.

Zoe peered over his shoulder. "They're right, it *is* going to get close – it's north-east of here now. Wow! We didn't reckon on it coming that near! But we'll avoid it if we don't go too far from shore. Any sign of Fingal?"

"The limpet's picking up a faint dolphin sound," answered Ben. "I'll see if it matches his call."

He tapped at the keyboard and punched the air as the result came up. "It's a match!" Ben stared at the expanse of blue water. "He's out there somewhere. He must be just within range."

"That's all very well." Zoe frowned. "But how are we ever going to catch up with him?"

"I don't know," said Ben thoughtfully.

"Unless…" He began to tap at the BUG keyboard again.

"Unless what?" asked Zoe.

"I've had a brilliant idea!" exclaimed Ben. "Do you remember the Mundo Marino website Uncle Stephen showed us?"

Zoe nodded.

"I had another look at it on the plane," Ben went on. "There was a load of info from when the park was well run, about how the dolphins were trained. And there was something we might be able to use to get Fingal to come to us."

"Really?" Zoe asked eagerly.

"The website said that if ever the barriers of the park pools were broken in a storm and the dolphins escaped out to sea, their trainers could set off a sort of pinger. The dolphins were trained to come to the sound straight away. Perhaps we could do the same."

Zoe's face fell. "You've forgotten something. We haven't got a pinger."

"The BUG can imitate one!" declared Ben, his eyes shining excitedly. "Why didn't I think of that before? I can set it to send out the call."

"How?" demanded Zoe. "We don't even know what it sounded like."

"That's where you're wrong, Captain," Ben told her. "There was a sound clip on the website. I remember thinking it sounded just like the timer on the cooker at home."

"We've certainly heard that often enough!" Zoe laughed. "But supposing the frequency is wrong. Or the interval between the pings. Then Fingal won't recognize it."

"I'll keep adjusting the sound till he does," said Ben firmly. "I know it's a long shot, Zoe, but it's our only chance of finding him."

"You're right," said Zoe. "It's worth a try! I'll keep the dinghy steady." She pulled out the first-aid kit. "After I've seen to your hand. We don't want to attract any more predators." She stuck a waterproof plaster over the cut.

A look of concentration on his face, Ben fiddled with the controls until he got the BUG's limpet to make a pinging sound. The children scanned the waves for the young dolphin.

"I'll try a different pitch," said Ben, after a few moments.

He tried setting after setting, but there was no sign of Fingal. Zoe adjusted the sails. A stiff breeze had got up and she had to work to keep the boat steady.

"It was a good idea," Zoe said. "But it's not working."

Ben's face was set. "We can't give up," he muttered through clenched teeth.

He adjusted the sound again. "Let's try that. Now it's time for lunch. I'm starving. Pass me one of those pastelitos."

They ate their pastries and fruit and washed them down with water. There was a fresh wind in their faces now and small clouds were scudding across the sky.

Zoe packed up the food and scanned the waves, desperately hoping to see some sign of Fingal.

"He's not going to come," she said at last. "I'll head us back just in case he's returned to the bay." She turned the dinghy towards San Miguel.

"Look!" shouted Ben suddenly. "What's that?"

A grey shape was speeding towards them through the water, leaping and plunging through the waves. It dived under the dinghy, flipping up its tail and sending a spray of water all over Ben and Zoe.

Now they could hear excited, high-pitched squeaks and the sleek round nose of a young dolphin burst up from the surface. It had a scar running down from its right eye.

"Brilliant, Ben," cried Zoe. "Your pinger worked. It's Fingal!"

CHAPTER EIGHT

Fingal swam round Ben and Zoe's dinghy, leaping happily in and out of the waves.

"He's really pleased to see us!" gasped Zoe in delight.

"He's showing us his tricks," said Ben, with a grin. "Look!"

With his next leap, the young dolphin gave a twist in the air, before plunging back into the waves. When he surfaced, he gazed eagerly at the children. Zoe clapped and whooped. This seemed to please Fingal. His following jump took in two elegant spins.

"I think that calls for a reward," said Ben. "On the website it said a whistle from the trainer means the dolphin's done well. They start with a whistle and food treats at the same time. Then they wean the dolphin off the food rewards so they respond just to the whistle."

Ben put his fingers to his mouth and blew a shrill whistle. Fingal immediately swam up to the boat and began to nod his head vigorously, making a loud chattering noise.

"He's only young." Zoe laughed. "I reckon he still links the whistle with food. Take the tiller while I give him a treat. Here, Fingal." She pulled a dolphin snack out of her backpack and lobbed it through the air. Fingal leaped up and took it cleanly.

"He seems to like it," said Zoe, as Fingal danced backwards across the waves on his tail. "He's showing us what he can do so we give him some more. Clever boy!"

"We'll run out at this rate," said Ben. "I'll try the whistle without the treat." He whistled again.

This time Fingal swam close and laid his head on the side of the dinghy next to Zoe's hand. She reached over and stroked his smooth, cold nose and the dome of his head.

"You are a lovely boy," she crooned, "and you'll soon be safe at the sanctuary."

"Keep him there if you can, Zoe?" said Ben, taking out his BUG and scrolling through the menu. "This is a great time to tag him with a tracking dart. Then we won't lose him again."

Ben aimed the BUG at Fingal. But at that moment a gust of wind caught him off guard and the dart embedded itself into the wooden side of the dinghy.

"Great!" Zoe laughed. "Now we'll be able to track our boat! Very useful."

Ben stuck out his tongue at her and aimed again.

This time the tiny dart flew home – straight into Fingal's back. The young dolphin didn't seem to notice at all.

He rolled playfully in the sea, and as Zoe bent over the side to stroke him again, he blasted her with water from his blowhole. He tossed his head back and chirped as if he was chuckling.

"That must be one of his tricks!" Ben laughed, as Zoe wiped her face.

"He likes all the attention," she said in delight. "We're getting his trust. Next task – take him somewhere that's safe and quiet and contact Uncle Stephen."

"There's an inlet a few miles away," said Ben, studying the satellite map on his BUG screen. "It's north-east of here. It seems remote – no houses or anything, but there's a small road leading down to it so the people from the Agua Clara Dolphin Sanctuary will be able to get a truck down there."

"Sounds ideal," said Zoe, moving back to her seat and settling herself with the tiller and sail ropes. "I'll sail and you keep an eye on Fingal. The odd treat should keep him with us."

Fingal swam round the boat, leaping among the waves.

Zoe smiled. "He's like a dog that knows it's going for a walk," she said.

Ben zoomed in on his map to get a close-up of the area. "Don't go too near the land," he warned. "The BUG's showing that the water soon gets shallow with hidden rocks. We don't want to run aground."

"No problem," said Zoe, turning the dinghy back out to sea and heading north-east.

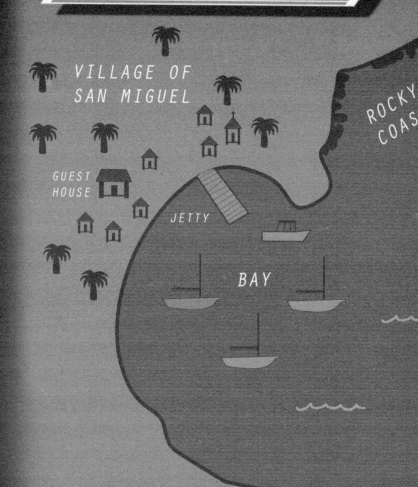

EDGE OF HURRICANE

N

CORAL ISLAND

not to scale

Fingal swam alongside the boat as it gained speed. Now and again, he would soar high in the air, twisting and turning before diving into the waves. Ben rewarded him each time with a whistle.

A sudden strong gust of wind caught Zoe in the face, taking her breath away. The boat lurched on the choppy swell.

"What's up with Fingal?" said Ben. "He's hanging back. Perhaps he's scared to stray into unknown waters."

The young dolphin had stopped metres behind the dinghy and was calling anxiously to them. Ben threw a dolphin treat into the water. Fingal watched as it fell, but didn't move forward to eat it. He edged backwards in the water, as if he was going to swim away at any minute.

"Come on, Fingal," said Zoe.

"I'll try his pinger," said Ben, pressing the buttons on his BUG.

He watched the sleek, rounded back of
the little dolphin, as he swam slowly up and
down just under the surface.

"We can't let him go back to the bay," he
said. "We've got no way of keeping him out
of the way of the fishing boats there."

Ben trailed a treat in the water. "He's
nosing at my hand."

"Good boy, Fingal," called Zoe.

There was a blast of wind across the bow. The sails flapped alarmingly and the boat lurched to one side. Zoe acted quickly to bring the dinghy round until the sails filled again and the boat steadied itself.

"Look ahead, Ben," she said anxiously. "I hope that's not the hurricane approaching. We know it was forecast to miss San Miguel, but we don't know how close it was going to come to the shore."

The two children peered at the horizon. Swelling waves were rolling in towards the shore, topped with white spitting flecks. Ominous clouds had appeared in the far distance.

"I reckon we're going to be caught if we stay here," said Ben grimly. "We've got to get Fingal to that inlet right now."

He turned to throw another treat into the water. But all he could see was the young dolphin speeding away from them.

"Fingal must have sensed the danger," he said. "If he's running away from the hurricane, then so should we."

CHAPTER NINE

Ben checked his BUG for Fingal's tracking signal. It showed an orange pulsing light moving swiftly through the water away from their dinghy, heading back the way they'd come.

"He's making for the bay," he said, worried. "And that could be dangerous. Any fishing boats will be making for San Miguel now, if the hurricane's getting closer."

Zoe pushed the tiller away and set a new course back towards the fishing village.

Ben checked his BUG again. "Fingal's signal shows he's swimming out to sea now, but at least he's heading south, away from the storm – and San Miguel."

Zoe brought the dinghy round and set a course to follow the little dolphin.

She glanced over at Ben's BUG. "I hope we can catch up with him. Dolphins can swim fast when they want to."

The clouds had spread across the sky now. As they sailed further from the shore the children could feel the wind growing stronger, making the dinghy lurch and dip violently.

Ben checked the BUG screen. "We're not getting any closer," he said.

"I'm trying to get us moving faster," said Zoe. "Hang on tight. Even though we're sailing away from the hurricane this wind's still getting fierce. I'm having a real fight to hold the tiller steady."

Ben called up the satellite forecast. "Bad news, I'm afraid," he said. "We're sailing right into the edge of the storm. It's going to be a bit wild here for a while."

Zoe yelped in surprise as a sudden gust nearly tore the mainsail sheet from her grasp. She could feel the first lashings of rain on her face.

"We'll have to get to shore," Ben shouted over the roaring wind.

"Too risky," Zoe shouted back. "We don't know if there are hidden rocks."

"You're the boss," answered Ben. "What do you want me to do?"

"Take the jib," she yelled. "Pull that sheet until the sail stops flapping. I'll deal with the rest."

Pulling on the jib sheet with one hand, Ben adjusted his BUG to set the pinger going at full volume. The sky was even darker now and the rain was hammering down.

"I'm keeping Fingal's signal going," he shouted over the sound of the wind and rain. "Dolphins have fantastic hearing."

The force of a high wave suddenly snatched the tiller from Zoe's hands.

"Look out!" she cried. "Duck!"

Ben threw himself down just in time, as the boom lifted and whipped across the boat with a crack.

The dinghy keeled over, the mast nearly touching the waves. Then, caught by the wind, it lurched over the other way, sending the children sprawling.

"We're out of control!" cried Zoe. "We've got to get the sails down – and fast. Take the tiller and steer into the wind if you can."

She scrambled over to the mast and released the mainsail, lowering it as fast as she could. Then she did the same with the jib.

Ben was struggling with the tiller. "I don't know how much longer I can hold on to this," he yelled, as the dinghy bucked and tossed in the waves.

"Don't worry," Zoe shouted. "It'll be better when we've got a sea anchor."

"But there isn't an anchor in the boat!" cried Ben.

"I know. I'm going to make one."

She pulled out the bailing bucket and untied the rope from its hook. She leaned out over the bow and tied the rope to the mooring handle right on the front of the boat.

"Have you gone mad?" shouted Ben. "That's no good as an anchor. It won't even reach the bottom."

"It doesn't have to," said Zoe. She heaved the bucket into the sea. Immediately the children felt the tug of the boat on the taut rope and it was blown round to face the oncoming waves.

They breathed a sigh of relief as the dinghy rode the next swell.

"A sea anchor creates a drag," Zoe

explained. "It makes us point into the wind and waves so we won't get blown around as much. When we learned about this on our course I never thought I'd be using it for real."

"I get it," said Ben. "The bucket's full of water so it acts like a sort of brake when the wind and water try to push the dinghy backwards."

"Exactly," replied Zoe, dashing the rain from her eyes. "Now we must both get down as low as possible and stay in the centre."

Ben lay down and scrabbled about in the bottom of the boat.

"What are you doing?" yelled Zoe.

"We should put our flippers on," Ben yelled back. "Just in case."

They'd just got them strapped to their feet when Ben glanced up. What he saw froze him to the spot.

A huge wave was speeding towards them, towering over the dinghy's prow, its top spraying with angry white foam.

Zoe could feel the swirl of a strong undercurrent trying to pull the dinghy round. It crested the next wave, and lurched so violently that she thought it would snap in half. Now they were plummeting into a deep trough and the huge wave was upon them. She gave a desperate pull on the tiller.

But it was too late. The boat was caught up by the fierce swell and the next minute it flipped sideways and turned right over. Zoe felt the whip of ropes and sails and managed to take a gasping breath before being flung into the dark, churning water.

Despite her life jacket, she was being tumbled around in the towering waves. No sooner did she feel air on her face than she was rolled back under.

Then at last a wave pushed her up and she felt herself bursting into the air. She breathed deeply and let herself float on the swell. She looked round desperately for her brother. But all she could make out were dark, ominous waves that lifted her up high and sucked her down again.

There was no sign of Ben.

CHAPTER TEN

"Ben!" shouted Zoe, hearing the panic in her own voice. "Ben! Where are you?"

A jumble of thoughts went round her head. Had her brother been swept further out to sea by the current? Had he jumped clear of the boat? Was he caught inside it, unable to free himself?

Zoe had a moment of cold, paralyzing horror. Wherever he was in this terrible sea, she had little chance of rescuing him.

She shook those fears away. She knew she had to try and find him. She scanned

the waves. It was a terrifying sight.
Each swell looked bigger than the one
before and the wind was blowing the rain
hard into her face until her cheeks stung.
The black clouds were still overhead,
making it so dark it was impossible to
see far.

And then a faint cry reached her. Zoe
pushed herself round in the water to see a
dark shape being thrown about in the
waves. It must be Ben!

Zoe struggled to make her way to him,
feeling herself being sucked back the whole
time by the currents. She could see Ben's
arms thrashing through the water. At last,
he was near enough for her to grab hold of
his life jacket.

"You're OK!" Zoe could scarcely get the
words out in her relief.

"Just about," shouted her brother over the
roar of the storm. "Now what?"

"Find the boat!" yelled Zoe. "We need something to hold on to."

"Won't it have sunk?"

"Flotation tank. Keeps it on the surface. And with any luck the backpacks will still be attached."

"So we just have to locate it then."

"Easy!" shouted Zoe. "You tagged it, remember."

"Brilliant!" Ben tried to punch the air and choked on a mouthful of water.

Zoe pulled her BUG out of the water, feeling a surge of relief that it was safely secured to her diving belt. She wiped her wet hair from her eyes and called up the tracking screen. "It's a long way off!" she called, watching the orange light in the water that marked the dinghy's position. "But we've got to try. This way."

Fighting the storm currents, they tried to make headway through the dark water.

Finally, Zoe slowed and trod water. "We're not getting very far," she panted. "I need a rest."

"Agreed," gasped Ben. They lay their heads back on their life jackets, holding hands to keep together, riding each wave.

"Is it my imagination or are the waves getting calmer?" said Ben, at last.

"You're right," said Zoe. "Look over there, there's a break in the cloud."

Ben looked up. Thin beams of sunlight could be seen filtering through the clouds.

"You've still got your BUG, haven't you?" asked Zoe.

"Safely tied to my belt," answered Ben. "But the limpet's with the boat – so there's no point in sending out a call to Fingal. He'd go there instead of coming to us."

"He's probably way off now," said Zoe, "but we can still check his tracking signal."

She had just got her hand round her BUG when the dark water swirled ahead and something heavy slammed into their legs. Ben and Zoe looked down in alarm.

A smiling dolphin face popped up from the waves in front of them, a scar running down from its right eye. It was Fingal. The young dolphin chirped loudly, walked backwards on his tail and then came swimming back to them.

Zoe stroked his side as he swam past.

"We're so glad to see you," she cried.
"Now the hurricane's moved on, you've
come to find us!"

Suddenly, the water all around them
began to seethe, and in an instant they
were surrounded by sleek grey bodies, arcing
and diving through the waves.

"It's a pod of dolphins," gasped Ben. "Fingal
seems to have made friends with them."

They could see Fingal leaping amongst
the group.

"They're getting a bit close for comfort,"
shouted Zoe, above the cries and chirps.
"They're circling us. I expect they're just
playing, but we'll have trouble getting past
them."

The dolphins were swimming right up to
Ben and Zoe now, forming a tight band
around them. They felt their arms and legs
being buffeted by the strong flippers.

Ben held out his arms to fend them off.

"I don't think they're playing," he said anxiously. "We should try and break through before we get hurt."

As a tail passed him, he kicked hard, hoping to burst through the gap, but at once another dolphin was on him, pushing him back to Zoe with its nose.

"I've got a bad feeling about this," he yelled. "Remember that programme about those dolphins that attacked seals and ate them?"

Zoe looked at him in horror. "We're in big trouble!"

CHAPTER ELEVEN

They tried to fend off the dolphins, pushing against the strong bodies.

"Fingal's still with them," cried Ben. "Look, here he comes. Surely *he* won't hurt us."

But the young dolphin began to join in with the jostling. The circle got even tighter.

"We're going to be crushed," shouted Zoe.

Suddenly, between the troughs in the waves, Ben could just see another fin cutting through the water towards them.

"There's a shark out there!" he exclaimed.

And now Zoe understood what the pod was doing.

"They're protecting us," she gasped. "Keeping the shark away. And Fingal's helping them."

Two of the dolphins peeled away from the pod and swam straight for the shark.

There was a tremendous splashing as the three huge creatures crashed together.

"What's happening?" yelled Ben.

"I can't see," Zoe yelled back. "They must be fighting it off."

Their dolphin guards continued to swim round them, Fingal giving the children a reassuring nudge with his nose as he passed.

Then Ben realized that the two dolphins were back. The pod was suddenly giving urgent chirps and squeaks.

"They must have chased it away," he shouted. "There's no sign—"

To Zoe's horror, he gave a cry and disappeared under the water.

The dolphins dived frantically. Zoe tried to follow, but the life jacket kept her on the surface. She tore at the straps, flung it off and dived, searching for her brother.

She could see him now and the blood turned to ice in her veins. The shark had swum under the pod and got its teeth firmly round one of Ben's flippers. It was shaking him like a rag doll. She swam down and tried to pull Ben away. But she was no match for the huge shark.

Then she remembered something she'd read about shark attacks. Hit it on the nose. She kicked down hard with her heel and whacked the shark just above its mouth. The shark recoiled, letting go of the flipper. Zoe grabbed Ben's life jacket and made for the surface as it lunged again, its mouth open wide, showing rows of sharp, deadly teeth.

Suddenly, something sleek and grey shot across and rammed the shark hard in the side of its face. It was Fingal. The shark reeled at the blow.

Ben's life jacket was pulling him up to the surface. Zoe swum up beside him.

"I didn't see it coming!" gasped Ben.

They peered anxiously into the depths. Dark shapes were flashing backwards and forwards in a desperate frenzy, as the other dolphins joined Fingal in attacking the shark.

"We need to get away from here," said Zoe urgently. "But how?"

A grey streamlined body pushed in between them and leaped into the air. It swam round and came up to them, a happy grin on its scarred face.

"It's Fingal!" exclaimed Ben.

Their young friend nudged them with his nose. Then he swam round and came up

behind them, lifting their arms as he passed.
He did it again.

"What's he up to?" said Ben.

"He wants us to take hold of his dorsal
fin," said Zoe. "I think he's going to give
us a tow. It's probably part of his training.
I hope he's got a destination in mind."

As Fingal went to pass them again, they
grasped his back fin, and at once felt his
strength and speed as he pulled them
through the water.

"I don't really care where we go," Ben
shouted back, spluttering a little as the
foamy waves splashed in his face. "As long
as it's far away from that shark."

Fingal swam strongly, keeping his fin just
above the surface of the water. Zoe's hand
began to feel numb from hanging on for so
long, but Fingal seemed tireless. Then a

worry began to form in her head.

"He's only ever lived in a pool," she called. "He could be swimming in circles."

"You're right," Ben called back. "But what else can we do? There's a hungry shark out there somewhere and..." He broke off and dashed the water from his eyes. "Can you see what I see?"

"What?" demanded Zoe, trying to peer ahead. "What is it?"

"Palm trees!"

"Is it the shore?" asked Zoe. She could see the tops of the green, frondy leaves now, the sun shining brightly on them through the widening gap in the clouds.

"It's the coral island," shouted Ben. "Fingal's brought us to safety."

The dolphin slowed a little way from where the island rose out of the sea. Ben and Zoe released his fin, and he disappeared, coming to the surface in an arcing dive a little way away. As the children swam towards the land, Ben peered down, marvelling at the wonderful colours of the coral beneath them.

"I win!" called Zoe, as she reached the shore.

She pulled off her flippers and stumbled out of the sea.

"Paradise!" she declared, throwing herself down on the sand underneath a palm tree.

"We'd better let Erika know where we are!" said Ben, getting out of the water and flopping down beside her. "Then she can contact Uncle Stephen and with luck the centre will come and get Fingal while he's still around here. We'll have to hide when they come, of course." He took his BUG and hit a hot key.

"Hello!" came Erika's voice. "What news?" Ben told her everything that had happened. "Fingal's here with us and he's tagged," he finished. "So if Uncle Stephen can call the Agua Clara Dolphin Sanctuary..."

"Will do," came Erika's calm voice. "Your BUG's giving me your location. I'll come and get you. We can retrieve your sailing dinghy later."

Ben stretched out on the sand. "No need to hurry!"

Erika laughed. "I'm afraid you can't be there when the sanctuary people turn up. See you soon." She rang off.

Ben jumped up and gazed out to sea.

"The pod's back," he cried. "Looks like they've seen off the shark."

The dolphins leaped and dived in the waves, which glittered in the sunshine.

"I wish we could thank them," said Zoe. "They saved our lives – with Fingal's help."

Fingal gave a series of calls and began to swim towards the pod. But then he whipped round and headed back towards the island. He chirped and walked backwards on his tail, as if he was in one of his shows back at the marine park.

"I've been thinking," said Ben. "It does seem a shame to have him taken to a sanctuary, no matter how good it is. He's getting used to the ocean and he seems to have found a pod without any help.

I reckon the best thing for him would be to stay in the sea with them."

"But how will we be sure he does stay with them?" Zoe sounded worried. "He could go back to bothering the fishing boats and get into danger."

The children watched Fingal diving in and out of the waves, clicking and chirping playfully at them.

"Maybe he is too used to people," sighed Ben. "Let's hope the sanctuary helps him change that behaviour."

Suddenly, the pod came closer to Fingal, calling and chirping. The young dolphin called back, nodding his snout.

"Go on, boy," said Zoe. "Go with them."

But Fingal swam closer to the island.

The pod kept up their calls. Then one of the larger dolphins broke away from the group and swam slowly towards Fingal. The children saw the two grey bodies dance round each other under the water.

"That's it, boy," urged Ben. "They won't hurt you."

The older dolphin made its way back to the pod. But Fingal still didn't follow. At last, the dolphins turned and headed off towards the deep ocean.

Then Fingal slipped underwater.

"Where's he gone?" asked Zoe anxiously. "I can't see him."

"There he is!" exclaimed Ben, pointing at a sleek shape moving like a torpedo towards the pod.

Zoe shielded her eyes. "Fingal's reached the other dolphins!" she cried. "Look, he's playing with them."

They watched as Fingal and his new family swam off into the distance.

"Better phone Erika again," said Ben, with a grin. "We're the only ones that need rescuing now."

CHAPTER TWELVE

Later that week, Zoe and Ben were lying in their garden, reading magazines. Gran was in the kitchen making one of her chocolate cakes to celebrate their successful mission.

Zoe turned to face Ben. "There's an article here about sailing," she said, with a grin. "Fancy some lessons?"

"Don't need them," declared Ben. "I could teach a class how to right a capsized dinghy. And how to bail it out!"

"You did well," said Zoe. "The boat hire woman had no idea what her dinghy had been through when we took it back."

Not long after Fingal had swum away with the pod, Erika had sped up to the coral island in a hired motorboat. They'd tracked down the capsized dinghy and Zoe had shown Ben how to stand on the keel to pull the vessel upright. The trusty bucket had proved very useful in bailing all the water out.

"Erika was really pleased with the response to Uncle Stephen's nets," said Zoe. "Especially in San Miguel – they were really keen to give them a go there."

"Especially that fisherman who started telling everyone about his encounter with the super-dolphin in the bay."

"The one that had teeth like knives and cut its way through his net?" Zoe laughed. "He'll be repeating that story for weeks. It was so funny I nearly forgot to pretend I didn't understand a word."

They heard the phone ring in the house. After a few moments, Gran poked her head out of the window. "That was your Uncle Stephen," she called. "He said it's urgent."

"Another mission so soon?" said Zoe, jumping up in surprise.

Gran shook her head. "No. He told me to turn the TV on right away!"

They ran inside and crowded round the little television in the kitchen. A news programme was on.

"And finally," said the newsreader, "a strange turn of events in the Caribbean. A group of wild dolphins have been entertaining tourists with their tricks."

The camera cut from the studio and swept over an expanse of blue water to show a pod of dolphins leaping in the waves.

Suddenly, two adult dolphins began to walk backwards on their tails.

A reporter appeared on screen. "I have Monica Vasquez from the Agua Clara Dolphin Sanctuary with me," he said. "Can you tell me what this is all about?"

A pretty, dark-haired woman came into shot. "There was a bottlenose dolphin from a marine park dumped in the sea," she told the camera. "We were alerted to his plight and were going to take him to the centre for rehabilitation. But very soon after that, we got a message saying that he'd been adopted by a local pod. They're teaching him how to live in the wild and it seems he is teaching them something, too."

The camera zoomed in as another dolphin reared up on its tail and walked backwards.

"See that scar under its eye!" cried Zoe, pointing to the screen. "It's Fingal!"

"He should have a better life now," said Ben. "Lots of fish whenever he wants them and no whistles to perform to. And although we needed that ride, I hope he never has to tow a human again."

"One thing's for certain," said Zoe. "He's found a home at last."

BOTTLENOSE DOLPHIN SURVIVAL

Bottlenose dolphins are found all over the world, in temperate and tropical waters.

No. of bottlenose dolphins living in the world today - not known, but they are not endangered.

Minimum world estimate ──────────────→ 470,000-690,000

No. of dolphins in the Gulf of Mexico alone (approx.) ──────→ 45,000

Life span: up to 20 years in the wild. There have been cases of dolphins living to 50, but this is very rare. Dolphins in good animal parks tend to live longer than those in the wild.

Dolphins are mammals. Unlike fish they give birth to live young, which they feed with their own milk.

They don't have gills either, and so cannot breathe underwater. They have to come to the surface every so often to take in fresh air. If they didn't, they would drown.

Dolphins are 2 to 3.9m in length. Their average weight is 150 to 200kg. Males are longer and much heavier than females.

Females breed once every two to three years. They are pregnant for twelve months. Calves are about 1 to 1.35m long and weigh 10-20kg. They are usually born tail first.

STATUS: LEAST CONCERN

The dolphin is not endangered as a species, but some regions' populations are under threat. Without dolphins, local ecosystems can be threatened.

RESCUE
BOTTLENOSE DOLPHIN FACTS

THREATS

FISHING

Some fishing nets are so big that they accidentally catch dolphins in them. Also, some areas are overfished so there is less food for dolphins to eat.

PREDATORS

Large species of shark, such as tigers and great whites, will prey on single adults and pups. Orca whales have also been known to attack dolphins. In Japan and in the Faroe Islands, dolphins are killed for food. Dolphin meat is sold in butcher's shops.

Dolphins give themselves names! Each dolphin has a signature whistle which is different for every dolphin. It helps them to identify each other. The mound of a dolphin's forehead is called the melon. A dolphin uses its melon to produce sound waves. When the waves echo back from an object, the dolphin can identify what the object is, its size, speed and even what sort of material it is made from. A burst of soundwaves from their melon can even stun a fish, so that they can eat it!

POLLUTION

Factory waste and farm fertilizers are washed into the sea and some of it can kill dolphins.

It's not all bad news!

The World Wide Fund for Nature is working with fishermen around the world to help them reduce the number of dolphins, sharks and turtles that they accidentally catch in their fishing nets. They are trying out different types of nets and other fishing equipment. A few countries have banned the hunting of bottlenose dolphins, and they have a special protected status in European law.

Following a massive earthquake, an orphaned giant panda has escaped from a sanctuary in China's Sichuan Province. Not only is he at risk of attack from leopards, but it seems he may have strayed into an area where all the bamboo has died. With the panda cub now in danger of starvation, it's up to Ben and Zoe to rescue him.

J. BURCHETT & S. VOGLER

WILD
RESCUE

FOREST FIRE

Ben and Zoe's latest mission takes them to South Borneo. An orang-utan has set up home on a palm oil plantation and is resisting all attempts to bring him to the safety of the nearby reservation. But when they discover that illegal logging has been taking place, it becomes clear that the orang-utan isn't the only one in grave danger.

Following reports of a polar bear shot dead near an Alaskan village, Uncle Stephen is sending Ben and Zoe to the scene. It seems that the dead bear had recently given birth. This means there are orphaned cubs out there. If Ben and Zoe don't get to them soon, the cubs won't stand a chance. But the young polar bears could be anywhere and there is a vicious storm brewing...

J. BURCHETT & S. VOGLER

WILD
RESCUE

SAFARI SURVIVAL

Ben and Zoe are off to a game reserve in the Kenyan savannah, where some tourists are paying big money to illegally hunt elephants for "sport". The latest visitor has his sights set on a mother and baby elephant… The race is on for Ben and Zoe to track down the vulnerable elephants before the hunters do. Will they get there in time?

Ben and Zoe's skills are put to the test when they are dispatched to the treacherous slopes of the Himalayas. Following an avalanche, a mother snow leopard and one of her cubs have been cut off from their territory, leaving her two other cubs to fend for themselves. It's down to the children to brave sub-zero temperatures and sheer rock faces, and lead the mother and her cub home.

If you want to find out more
about bottlenose dolphins, visit:

www.wdcs.org
www.orcaweb.org.uk
www.dolphincareuk.org
www.wwf.org.uk